Novels by Kelly Cheek

All We Hold Dear

Trial by Fire

The Lost Colony

JackSimile and the Phantom Fury

Spirit Breather

The Piper

The SpiritSense Trilogy

In Restless Dreams

First Light

When We Were Gone Astray

The Facebook Trilogy

Profile

Private Messages

Poked

Kelly Cheek

ISBN: 978-1-7335022-7-6

Published by
Fiery Muse Publishing, LLC
PO Box 630702
Highlands Ranch, CO 80130

Printed in the United States of America

This book began life with only five chapters several years ago, after which I subsequently lost interest in it. It spent its stunted infancy languishing on my computer until a few months ago when a brief conversation with my muse rekindled my interest.

Now fully-grown, I dedicate this book, as I do so many others, to my muse, my lovely wife, Linda.

Chapter 1

Long ago, Hayley Hoffmann had trained herself to recognize the specific kinds of knocks that sounded on her door, and the reasons behind them. Collection agency representatives, for example, had a firm, authoritative knock, backed up as it was by the rule of law. On the other hand, friends often knocked more softly. There were, of course, numerous minute variations, an endless spectrum of nuances relative to the individuals doing the knocking, and their personalities.

The fact that she was wrong as often as she was right didn't deter her from believing in her ability.

Part of her ability was due to her experience as a music teacher, and her habit of listening closely for alterations in pitch, tone and modulation. A large part of it, though, was due to past experience.

The knock that sounded on her door now was of the authoritative variety, though not quite as forceful. Not that it really mattered anymore. The collection agency knocks hadn't come in years, not since she was a girl living with her mother. But old habits, as they say . . .

She looked through the peephole, but didn't recognize the man standing there. He was wearing a suit and tie, with a conservative haircut. She pushed her golden hair back over her shoulder and opened the door.

"Hayley Hoffmann?" he asked.

"Yes," she said with a smile and a friendly tone.

"Ah," he said, pulling a large envelope from a briefcase. "I'm with Harrison, Jenkins and Morrow. I was instructed to deliver this to you." She took the envelope, looking at it curiously, and the man pulled out a pad and pen. "And if you could just sign this."

She saw that it was simply an acknowledgment of receipt. She signed it and gave him back the pen.

"Thank you," he said. "Have a nice day."

"Thanks. You too," she smiled again.

Hayley closed the door and looked at the envelope. It was boldly emblazoned with the self-important logo of the Harrison, Jenkins and Morrow law firm. The name was familiar, but she wasn't sure why. She didn't have a lawyer, hadn't needed one. She plopped down on her sofa and ripped open the envelope. Inside were a few sheets of paper. The first was a typed letter.

Elsbeth Huber
Garbsener Landstraße
30419 Hannover, Germany

Hayley Hoffmann
4315 Raleigh Street
Denver, Colorado 80212

Dear Ms. Hoffmann,

I am Elsbeth Huber. I was a companion of your father Baldric Hoffmann for several years. I do not know if you knew (and if you did not, I am sorry I let you know this way) but your father passed away in 2020.

As a nurse, I attended to his medical needs for several years until he died. Yes, I was his caretaker, but I was also his friend. Towards the end of his life he told me that he had a daughter in the United States, but he had not had contact with her for the 24 years when he left America.

I am sorry it took so long to find you. I am afraid your father was not a good accountant or businessman. After his death, much time was spent paying off his debts and sorting out his belongings. In the end, there was little money left, but most of what was left was left to me. While I appreciate some of the things he gave me, I have little use of most of them.

Although Baldric had not named any relatives in his will, I remembered him speaking of you and I took it upon myself to look for you. My efforts were rewarded a month ago, so I have prepared this information to send to you.

The above address in Hanover Germany is your father's house, which I believe should be yours. Do not hesitate to contact me if you have any questions or would like to collect your estate.

With best regards,
Elsbeth Huber

p.s. My English is not so good. I hope you could understand.

Hayley sat back and looked at the letter, unsure how to feel about it. She had vague memories of her father, or rather, she had vague memories of when her father had been there. He left when she was six, and she never heard from him after that.

She put the letter aside and looked at what was under it, mainly just numerous legal forms, including a copy of her father's will. Essentially, what was left to Elsbeth Huber was everything in the house, or at least everything that was left after some items had been repossessed or sold to satisfy creditors. She didn't see anything about the house itself, except for the fact that it was where the other items were located.

The last item was a photograph of her father. The man looked old and wasted away. Nothing about him was familiar to Hayley. His face appeared almost deformed, as if he had experienced a massive stroke and half of it didn't work anymore.

She got up to look for her phone. She was always laying it down somewhere and forgetting where she left it. After spending a couple of minutes searching, she found it on the music rack of her piano. She pulled up the keypad and her mother's number appeared on top. She pressed the little green telephone receiver icon, and she heard the tone of the phone ringing on the other end.

"Hello, honey," came the answer.

"Hi, Mom. Guess what I got."

"I don't have a clue."

"My father's house in Germany."

"Huh?"

"Did you know he died two years ago?"

"No," her mother replied, her voice suddenly very quiet. "I haven't heard anything from your father since he left all those years ago. Wait, you're saying he left you his house?"

"Not exactly." Hayley told her briefly about the envelope she received from the law firm, and about the letter from Elsbeth Huber.

"Well, I guess that's something. At least he thought of you at some point, enough to mention you to this nurse." Neither of them spoke for a few moments. Finally, her mother broke the silence. "So, honey, what are you going to do?"

"I think I'm going to go to Germany."

"Just like that?"

"Why not?" Hayley asked. "Summer vacation starts in a couple of weeks. For the next three months, I have plenty of time and no plans."

"Yeah, but Germany?"

"Well," Hayley retorted "again, why not? I've heard Germany's beautiful. I've never been there, and I'd love to visit and see what it's like. Now, it turns out I have a house there."

"And I suppose there must be some curiosity about your father."

"There is definitely some of that. I probably won't find any answers as to why he left, but maybe I can, at least, get an inkling of what he was like."

"Well," her mother said, "I can tell you why he left."

"What?"

"I mean, not in great detail, but I can give you the broad strokes." She spoke tentatively, choosing her words carefully. "He was saving himself. Your father," she took a deep breath, "he wasn't an honest man. He was an investor, and was good at convincing other people to hand over their money.

"But it turned out that he was skimming money from their investments, and keeping it for himself. When some of those investments started going bad, some of the investors wanted out, but their money was gone. When news got out, others wanted to cash in, too. But even with investments that were doing well, he couldn't come up with their money.

"We weren't happy," she added quietly. "Our time together was really quite tense. Part of that, I have to admit, could have been his national origin. The German persona often seems harsh to Americans. I mean, at first, he seemed almost exotic to me, and he was attentive so, to me, it was romantic.

"But in time, he seemed to change. We fought frequently. I realized afterwards that the change was probably due to his financial house of cards being on the verge of collapse. So, before the inevitable storming of the castle, he left. He just packed up all of his things and was gone before I knew it."

"And after he left," Hayley said, "that's when all the collectors came calling."

"That's right."

"Mom, I'm thirty years old. Why is it you never told me about this before?"

"I told you a little."

"You told me it wasn't because of me, since little kids often feel responsible for their parents' breakup."

"I don't know, honey. You were little when it happened, so you wouldn't have understood anything about it. And I didn't want to pollute any memory you might have had of him. By the time you were older, well, it was all in the past. I just didn't see any point in dredging it up again."

"But don't you see, Mom? All this time, I thought *you* were the financially irresponsible one. Whether I initially felt responsible or not, I don't really remember. But as I grew older, I knew my father left us, so any memory I had of him was already polluted. He never had any contact with me, so whatever memories I may have had eventually faded away. But I have vivid memories of the collection agencies calling at our home."

"Well, maybe it wasn't the best decision," her mother conceded. "But maybe this trip will help you fill in some of the blanks."

Chapter 2

The last two weeks of school passed quickly. As an elementary school music teacher, Hayley loved her kids. Holding their attention could sometimes be an issue, but once they started recognizing the power they had to actually make music, she could usually get them to focus.

Her bubbly personality and her own childlike sense of wonder drew people, especially children, to her, and to many of them, she was their favorite teacher. When the classroom experience was as interesting and as lively as she was able to make it, time passed quickly.

Her evenings in those last two weeks were spent in a sort of tunnel vision, as she prepared for her trip. She had called Elsbeth to let her know she was coming and to make arrangements to meet her when she arrived. On the phone, Elsbeth sounded warm and personable, and Hayley liked her immediately.

The flight was long, with a brief stop in New York and a change of planes in Amsterdam, and it felt good to finally get off the plane in Hannover. After a sixteen-hour flight and an eight-hour time zone gain, it was now Sunday morning, exactly one day later from when she left Denver, though it felt like the middle of the night to her.

It was only a twenty minute taxi ride from the airport to the house. Hayley didn't have a lot of reference, so she had been picturing a quaint little alpine bungalow, alternating with images of dour concrete bunkers.

The house, standing behind a stone wall, was a very old and stately half-timbered building, three stories tall, with the third story set into the high-peaked red-tiled roof. As Hayley looked at it, she felt the breath pulled from her lungs. The ancient-looking building caused a physical reaction in her that she couldn't explain.

It was set back from the road in a wooded area. The grand house was mostly white, but with dark exposed

15

vertical and horizontal timbers, and crisscrossing diagonal timbers under the windows. As the taxi drove away and Hayley approached the front door, the door opened. An attractive woman around sixty years old stood there. She had tired-looking eyes, but a ready smile.

"Hayley," she said, "it is good to meet you." Her German accent was so strong, it was difficult for Hayley to not picture Frau Blücher from *Young Frankenstein*.

"You too, Elsbeth. Thank you for meeting me here."

Hayley put her bags down on the floor inside the door. Despite the cheery look of the house from the outside, the interior was dark. Hayley noticed that the heavy drapes were pulled closed on most of the windows. But Elsbeth began remedying that after she closed the door.

"I apologize," she said, "I had hoped to get here earlier, but I had a patient to check on who required more of my time." She pulled the drapes aside in the front room, and sunlight flooded in. The room was white, with dark and heavy exposed timbers, giving it a look that made Hayley think of a Swiss chalet, despite the size of the place.

"Please sit," Elsbeth said, indicating the sofa in front of the window. Hayley eagerly sat down. She had been sitting for many hours, but she was so tired, it felt good to get off her feet again. Elsbeth sat in a chair opposite her.

"I am so sorry about your father," she said.

"Oh, Elsbeth," Hayley replied empathetically, "I didn't know my father. I'm sorry about your friend."

Elsbeth smiled sadly, emphasized by the fatigue showing in her eyes.

"I suppose I should tell you," she said quietly, "Baldric was more than my friend. He was my patient, of course, but in time, we became friends. As we came to know each other, though, the friendship became . . . more."

"I thought so," Hayley smiled. Elsbeth tilted her head and frowned. "He left everything to you," Hayley explained. "I figured it was more than just friendship."

"It may not be exactly what you think," Elsbeth replied. "By the time I knew him, he was not able to be - physical. He had tried to kill himself."

"Oh my god," Hayley said. Never having known her father, her remark was more for Elsbeth.

"Things were not going well for Baldric. I suppose one could say he deserved what was happening to him." She spoke slowly, and her eyes wandered as she spoke, as if she were constantly searching for the correct English words, sometimes pausing when they didn't come immediately. "He had done things that were illegal and un—" another pause, "unethical."

Echoes of what Hayley had learned from her mother.

"I do not know details of what he did, but the executor of his will later told me he built up a fortune by cheating others out of their money. It eventually caught up with him. A few years ago, he was married to a woman who seemed to love him, and he thought the world of her. But she turned on him. She sued him for everything she could get.

"That was in 2008. When the recession struck, he lost much of his money. His wife got what she could, but it was not as much as she had hoped."

"Interesting," Hayley said. "I guess I never realized that 2008 had an effect outside of the United States."

"Oh yes, it was bad here, too," Elsbeth nodded. "Somehow he kept the house and many of the things in it. But still, he lost so much, and people were coming after him. It became too much for him, so he shot himself in the head."

"He shot himself in the head?" Hayley asked with a disbelieving tone. "And he survived?"

"He survived, but he was not the same as before. He needed to learn again how to walk and talk. He had a caretaker who helped him relearn how to do the most basic things. It was during this—" a long pause, "rehabilitation time that I met him. At first, he just looked at me. He could not speak.

"Well, as time passed, he regained some of his strength, and the caretaker's time was reduced. When the caretaker was not there, I would come over if I had the time. I helped Baldric get some of his strength back, and do the things that other adults take for granted. And during that time, we became friends.

"But there were some abilities that he never regained. And he was very depressed. As time passed and his mood became darker, I asked a friend who is a psychiatrist to see him. Baldric resisted, but some of it, apparently, got through. It helped a little.

"But from what he told me about himself and his life, he was never again like he had been before. Still, our friendship deepened. He seemed to be better when we were together. Oh, the darkness was always there, just below the surface, but it *stayed* there, in the background, when I was with him. To this day, I do not know if that was because he expended special effort for my sake, or if it was due to some effect I had on him." She smiled a sad smile.

Hayley smiled back at her in return. She could easily imagine Elsbeth having such a calming effect on someone.

"But, unfortunately, it was not enough. My mother died and I had to go to Berlin for two weeks. That was in 2018. When I returned, he had shot himself again."

"Oh, Elsbeth," Hayley said, hurting for her.

"I had asked a friend to look in on him while I was gone. She is the one who found him. I did not even know he still had a gun. But again, it did not kill him. Not right away. He lingered for two years after that, but he was never the same as even when I knew him."

"I'm so sorry."

Elsbeth smiled her sad smile and shook her head.

"Thank you." She took a deep breath and exhaled it, as a cleansing breath, clearing out the memories.

"You mentioned this house," Hayley said hesitantly.

"I was very surprised when he wanted to give it to me."

"It's beautiful," Hayley said, looking around. "I love old architecture with character."

"It is yours now," Elsbeth said. "The deed is here," she pointed to a folder on the coffee table in front of Hayley, "and other important papers."

Hayley looked back at her and shook her head.

"But I didn't see anything about the house in the copy of the will you sent."

"No, that was an earlier arrangement. Your father wanted me to have the house. I think he knew that he was not to be here much longer. Looking back, I realize that he probably also knew that the house would be lost after his death, when knowledge of his illegal activities became known." Elsbeth took a deep breath before continuing. "It was just a few months before my mother died, he sold me the house for ten euros, and he signed it over to me. It was a legal transaction, so it is mine to give."

"That is so generous of you," Hayley said. "Are you sure about this?"

"Oh, Hayley, I have a very nice home. Here, there are memories of Baldric. Many of them were good, but there were many bad ones, too. If I stayed here, I would see his ghost everywhere I looked. For you, there are no such memories."

"You're a very kind woman," Hayley said. "I can certainly see what he saw in you."

"Well," Elsbeth said, taking another breath and looking around. She looked back at Hayley and followed a different thought. "It is a very long way from America. You must be exhausted."

"I really am," Hayley admitted.

"Come with me. I will show you to the kitchen and the bathroom and a bedroom, and then I will leave you to get some rest."

Elsbeth led Hayley toward the back of the house into a modern, beautifully-appointed kitchen.

"There is food in the refrigerator and in the pantry here," she pointed. "Dishes are there, glasses there."

"Elsbeth, honestly! You certainly didn't have to stock the kitchen!"

"Eh," Elsbeth shrugged and pointed to a door. "The garage is through there. The car is yours, too. The title is in the folder with the other papers." Hayley shook her head and sighed.

From the kitchen, Elsbeth led Hayley to the stairs. The bannister and steps were made of the same dark wood as the exposed timbers. On the other side of the stairway, the entire east side of the house was an expansive ballroom.

At the top of the stairs, Elsbeth indicated a room on the right. "Here is a bathroom." Continuing down the hallway, she paused for a moment, and touched a door on the left. She looked at Hayley. "This was Baldric's room. This is your house, so you may sleep there if you like, of course. But if not, the bed in this room next to it is ready."

"Thank you, Elsbeth. I think I'll check out my father's room later."

Elsbeth's face, Hayley thought, looked almost relieved.

"Well," she said, "I will leave you now."

On an impulse, Hayley reached out and pulled Elsbeth to her and held her for a few moments in a firm hug. When she let go of her, Elsbeth looked at her, her eyes swimming in tears.

"Well," she said again, blinking them away, "I will leave you now." But she smiled warmly at Hayley before she turned and went back down the stairs.

As she went down, Hayley saw her wipe her eyes.

Chapter 3

It was nearly 6:00 in the evening when Hayley woke up. She was a little chagrined, knowing that she would likely have a hard time sleeping that night.

She decided it was time to explore this house, her father's house.

Her house.

She started with her father's room, the one next to hers. She pushed the door open and went inside. The curtains were closed and the room was dark, so the first thing she did, to dispel the ghost that Elsbeth had mentioned, was to open the curtains and let some light in.

The bed was large and masculine, and made from, apparently, the same dark wood as so many other parts of this house. Hayley sat down on the bed and looked at the bedside table. There were a couple of books there which, in German, she didn't recognize. Under the lamp, there was a silver-colored frame with a photograph in it. A photograph of Hayley sitting in her father's lap when she was five or six years old.

Tears filled her eyes as she picked up the photo and looked at it. She had no memory of the moment immortalized in the picture, but the face of her father was happy. It was the face that she recalled in those few vague memories she had of him.

She wondered if, in that moment, she was the cause of his happiness, or if she was only incidental. And she remembered Elsbeth's similar comment about *her* effect on him. Hayley found herself wondering what to do with this new information, this image of a father she didn't know.

She was saved, for the moment, at least, from giving it further consideration when her stomach reminded her that she hadn't eaten anything in a long time. The little packet of pretzels on the last plane hardly counted. She placed the picture back on the table and left her father's room.

Downstairs in the kitchen, Hayley opened the pantry and was bewildered by the variety of food items that she didn't recognize. Her stomach growled again, and she decided to check the refrigerator to see if there was anything already prepared.

Everything there was also, naturally, labeled in German, but she could, at least, recognize the food itself. Some of it, anyway. There was a plastic container of something called *Kartoffelsalat*. Hayley opened the top and smelled it. It was potato salad, though different from the potato salad she was familiar with back home.

Finding a spoon, Hayley scooped some out into a bowl. Besides the potatoes, she tasted onion, vinegar and bacon. Paired with a little *Geflügel-Fleischwurst*, her stomach was satisfied for a while.

Fortified to continue her exploration, she continued her self-guided tour on the first floor and found herself in a room with floor-to-ceiling bookshelves, and each of the shelves was almost entirely filled. A small table with two chairs was in one corner, a comfy-looking sofa with an end table in another, promising that this library would be a welcoming place to read.

A brief circuit of the room revealed that, while most of the titles were in German, a few were not. She recognized several classics, both fiction and non-fiction, and a few modern volumes, in English. She determined that this room definitely merited closer examination.

At the back of the house, she discovered the large garage that Elsbeth had pointed to, large enough for four or five cars. There was only one car in it, but it was a beauty. She recognized the BMW logo above the front grill, but the car was different from any BMW she had seen. The convertible was bright red, sleek but curvy, kind of reminiscent, she thought, of a late-fifties Corvette.

There were six bedrooms and four bathrooms on the second floor, including the *en suite* bathroom off the master bedroom. The third floor was essentially an expansive attic. It was divided into several rooms, additional bedrooms, perhaps, but there was no furniture in them. They were apparently only used for storage of unused items. There was also a basement, with more items in boxes.

Near the bottom of the basement stairs was a modern-looking door. She turned the handle and pulled it open. There was, she thought, a slight hiss, as if she had broken a seal, and she went inside to find a voluminous fully-stocked wine cellar. She walked the length of the room, overwhelmed as she looked down several rows of wine racks.

Hayley's initial tour of the house complete, she felt a little bewildered. At some point, she knew she would have to go through all the boxes and trunks stored in the attic and the basement, to determine what should be kept and what should be sold or donated to charity. But the sheer volume of the stuff made it seem an onerous task. She certainly didn't feel like it now.

By this time, only one thing sounded good to her. She went to the kitchen and poured a glass of the Riesling she had seen in the refrigerator earlier, and she carried it to the library. In her earlier tour of the room, she had noticed a volume of Robert Frost poetry. She retrieved that book and settled on the sofa, prepared to relax for a few minutes with some of her favorite verses.

§

It was after 9:00 when she opened her eyes, the last verse she had read lingering in her memory:

> Let the night be too dark for me to see
> Into the future. Let what will be, be.

She sat up and stretched and looked around the room, as if getting her bearings. She picked up her glass and swallowed the last of the Riesling, and she got up to put the book back in its place on the shelf. But she didn't feel sleepy. Her long sleep in the morning and her nap now had left her refreshed and awake enough that she figured it would be a few hours before she could fall asleep again.

She stood there pondering what she wanted to do, and she remembered the wine cellar. The Riesling she had this evening was excellent, and she was curious about what other varieties and vintages might be available. Plus, there was something else that was bothering her about the wine cellar, some little detail that seemed out of place, but she couldn't quite recall.

She went down to the basement and through the door into the sealed wine cellar. When she got there, though, it occurred to her that, while she liked wine, she didn't know much about it. The labels, especially the German ones, meant nothing to her.

Haley wandered up and down the aisles of wine racks looking at the bottles, some of them, apparently, quite old. She was bewildered by the impressive inventory, even if she didn't know anything about the wines themselves. When she reached the end of the racks, in the back corner, she still hadn't found what had been tickling her brain.

She went back to the front of the room, where the door was located, and she walked along just looking down the rows of racks as she had earlier. When she got to the end, she saw it. All of the racks were so neat, so precisely-placed. Yet in the last row, one rack down on the end was slightly out of place. It had been imperceptible when she was standing in front of it moments before, but looking down the row, it was easy to see how the last one stuck out at a slight angle.

Standing in front of it now, Hayley pushed it toward the wall, and she was surprised at how easily it moved. At about five feet tall, and filled with bottles, she expected to have to push hard to get it to move. But it moved with little resistance, and it didn't scrape on the floor at all. When it came up against the wall, she heard a click, and the rack stayed in place.

Following the sound, she looked under the second row of bottles and found a little metal device, a clip of some kind. She reached under the row and felt the clip, finding how it moved, and she unfastened it again.

The rack moved on a hidden hinge attached to the rack beside it, and Hayley easily pulled it out away from the wall. Except that there was no wall behind the rack. There was a door. The coloring and texture was the same as the wall, but a small handle, hidden when the rack was in place, was now visible.

A special stash? she thought. She turned the handle and pushed the door open, almost expecting to find herself in something like the set of an Indiana Jones movie. She felt around inside the door and found a switch. The light was dim, but enough to see by.

There were only a couple of shelves on the wall, with a few items on them, a little dusty, but not as much as she had expected. They appeared to be antiques. One of them was a large brass compass, mounted in a wooden box on a gimbal which allowed it to remain upright in any position. She recalled one of her vague memories about her father and his interest in nautical paraphernalia.

There were a couple of old books which, since they were German, she didn't recognize. And next to them, there was a box of clear plastic or Lucite. Inside it was a book, the exact dimensions of the interior of the box, but this book looked much older than the other two. Where the top met the bottom portion of the box, she could see a rubber seal. The box wasn't locked, but was held closed by a metal clasp on each side. Easy enough to open, but Hayley was still hesitant to open it. Nonetheless, she was intrigued.

She had seen a copy of the Gutenberg Bible at the New York Public Library, printed in the 1450s. She remembered being fascinated that a book so old had survived for so long. It was incomplete, but she knew there were a few complete copies in various places around the world.

The book enclosed in this Lucite box intrigued her just as much as that Bible had. What was it? How had it survived all these years? And did she dare open the box to get a better look at the book inside?

§

Hayley picked up her phone from the table beside her bed. It was 1:00 in the morning and, as she suspected, she hadn't been able to fall asleep yet.

She realized that she hadn't called her mother after she arrived, and immediately felt guilty about that. She did a quick internet check and found that it was only 5:00 p.m. in Denver.

"Hi Mom," she said when her mother answered. "Sorry I haven't called before now."

"That's okay, honey. How are you doing?"

"I'm just really messed up timewise. Bad case of jetlag. I slept for several hours after I got here this morning, and now, it's one o'clock in the morning, and I'm lying here wide awake."

"Aw, I'm sorry. Well, how's it going otherwise?"

"Great! Elsbeth is the sweetest person. Not at all what I expected. The house is beautiful. In fact, I think it might be more accurate to call it a mansion."

"Really?"

"Well, maybe not, but it's certainly a lot more grand than my little bungalow. It's big and really old. Oh, and there's an incredible library in here, even though it's mostly German and I don't know what most of the books are. There's an amazing wine cellar, and a few antiques that have me absolutely flabbergasted.

"By the way, my father was into nautical things, wasn't he?" she asked.

"Uh, some," her mother replied, drawing out the syllables as she thought about it. "Mostly, it was just old things. He really liked mementos from the past."

"Hmm," Hayley mused.

"I remember he said he always felt like he was born in the wrong century."

"Interesting." Her head was swimming with the things she had seen and learned, and she didn't know what else to say. "Well, I should probably try to get to sleep, despite my body's current resistance. But I just wanted to let you know I got here alright."

"I'm glad you did. It was good to hear from you."

Hayley hung up and put her phone back on the table. The final verse of another poem that she had read earlier went through her mind.

> The woods are lovely, dark and deep,
> But I have promises to keep,
> And miles to go before I sleep,
> And miles to go before I sleep.

But she was asleep before the verse left her mind.

Chapter 4

Hayley discovered that the bedroom she was sleeping in faced east. The discovery was made when a blazing shaft of sunlight found its way through the window and crawled directly across her face.

Note to self, she thought grumpily, *close the curtains before going to bed tonight!*

She sat up and stretched, and she glanced down at her phone. It was only 5:10.

Even though she had only gotten four hours of sleep, though, she felt fairly refreshed. It was especially an improvement over yesterday morning. And she suddenly felt restless to investigate some of the things she had discovered last night.

She did a cursory search through the kitchen and the pantry and couldn't find any tea. She was mildly disappointed about that. She would do a more thorough search some other time. For now, the orange juice (*orangensaft*) she found in the refrigerator would do. She found some bread rolls (*Brötchen*) and some kind of ham (*Schwarzwälder*), and that served as her breakfast.

She would have to do a more in-depth study on German food, in order to know what to do with so many of the things in the kitchen.

Now that her hunger had been satisfied, she pulled her hair back into a loose braid while she thought about what she wanted to do. The library seemed like a good place to start, but since the majority of the books were in German, she figured that she would need the help of somebody who spoke German to even know what she had.

Thinking about the books, though, recalled to her mind the little alcove off the wine cellar, the hidden room where she saw that old book in the Lucite box. The apparent antiquity of the book intrigued her immensely, and she realized with no small surprise that she shared the feeling that her father had. While she wouldn't go so far as to say that she had been born in the wrong century, she had long had a great love of things from the past.

Standing in front of it now in the little room in the wine cellar, she felt that tingly feeling she remembered feeling at the New York Public Library a few years before when she saw the Gutenberg Bible. With shaky hands, she picked up the Lucite container and carried it out of the room. She wouldn't open it. She knew that, for a book this old, temperature and humidity levels were important to keep at a controlled level. But she wanted to be able to look at it in better light than the dim light of the alcove.

She carried it upstairs and placed it on the kitchen counter, looking at it from every angle. God, if only she could open it and leaf through it! Still, she knew it would likely be in German and would mean nothing to her, anyway.

Hayley decided to call Elsbeth. Maybe she knew something about the book. Grumbling at herself about having misplaced her phone again, she took off through the house looking for it. She finally found it in the bathroom where she had washed her face and brushed her teeth that morning. She found Elsbeth's number and called it.

"Hello, Hayley," she answered in her Frau Blucher voice. "How are you doing?"

"Fine, thanks. Are you able to talk?"

"Yes, for a couple of minutes." It sounded like she was in her car. "I am between patients."

"I found a very old book encased in a Lucite container down in the basement. Do you know anything about it?"

"No, I am afraid I do not. I never went down into the basement."

"Hmm," Hayley replied, clearly disappointed.

"What is it?" Elsbeth asked. "Is there anything on the cover?"

"The cover looks like really old, really dark leather. There are some markings on it, but I can't make it out. It looks like it's actually carved into the leather." The disappointment was thick in her voice. "Oh well," she sighed, "it's probably old German and wouldn't mean anything to me anyway. I'm just so curious."

"I know of someone who might be able to help you," Elsbeth said. "A few years ago, I had a patient who was dying of cancer. Her son is a professor of history at Stotzheim University. His name is Schiller. Max, I think."

"Max Schiller?"

"I think so. He sounded like you. He loved old things. He was passionate about history."

"Stotzheim University," Hayley repeated. "Okay, I'll give it a try. Thank you!"

Hayley pulled up the browser on her phone and did a quick search. Stotzheim University came up right away, and she found the phone number.

"Stotzheim Universität," said a woman's voice.

"Do you speak English?" Hayley asked.

"A little, yes."

"Is Professor Schiller there?"

"Uh, Professor Schiller is here today at 9:00. His first class is at 10:00."

"Thank you," Hayley replied. She hung up and looked at the time. It was just after 8:00. She mapped a route from her current location to the university. It was only about fifteen minutes away.

§

Hayley decided that the bright red 1958 BMW 507 convertible was a keeper. It performed beautifully, and looked great in the process.

She arrived at the university at 8:40. After making contact with a couple of people, she found one who understood enough English to be able to direct her to Schiller's office. She was standing outside his locked door at 8:55, anxiously watching in the direction she had come from for someone who looked like a history professor.

"Guten Morgen. Kann ich dir helfen?"

She quickly turned in the direction of the soft voice and found a man looking curiously at her, having come from the other direction. In his late thirties, his ash-blond hair was a little tousled, his hands were full of books, a battered briefcase and his keys.

"Oh," she said, surprised, "Professor Schiller?"

"Ja."

"Do you speak English?"

"I do, yes," he replied with a bit of an accent. He smiled as he fumbled his key into the lock and opened the door. He looked briefly at the Lucite box she was holding as he passed. "Come in."

"Thank you." Hayley followed him into his office. The small room was full of books, and he placed the ones he was carrying on his desk. He motioned toward a chair in front of his desk, and Hayley sat down. "Professor Schiller, my name is Hayley Hoffmann."

"I am pleased to meet you, Hayley Hoffmann. You may call me Max." He sat down behind his desk and sighed. Listening to his relaxed, soft-spoken voice, Hayley wondered if he ever had trouble keeping his students awake. "You are English?"

"American. I'm from Denver, Colorado."

"Ah. Well, what can I do for you?"

"Elsbeth Huber suggested I talk to you." Max looked up in the air as he tried to place the name. "She's a nurse. She said she cared for your mother."

"Ah, yes," he said.

"I'm so sorry about your mother."

"Thank you," he said softly, even softer than before. Just for a moment, she wondered if she saw tears in his eyes.

"I have an old book that I'd like to see if I could get some information about. Two things, though: I don't speak

32

or read German, and I don't want the book to disintegrate into a pile of dust."

He smiled and looked down again at the Lucite box in her lap.

"Is that the book?"

"Yes, it is," she replied as she handed it to him. Keeping the box closed, its rubber seal intact, he looked carefully through the Lucite at the front cover, the back cover, the spine and the edges of the pages. He picked up a magnifying glass and looked more closely at a few areas. He glanced back up at Hayley, his eyes twinkling.

"Can you see what it says?" Hayley asked.

"I do not think so," he said, looking back down at it. "The tooled leather looks like it may have been scuffed and scraped a long time ago. Those marks have aged with the tooling. It is difficult, now, to tell for certain where the original tooling ends and these other marks begin. And it is very ornate, as well, so that makes it even more difficult. But it could be Middle Low German. However, I am afraid that is only a guess."

"Middle Low German?" Hayley repeated.

"German language that dates as far back as the early thirteenth century." He looked back up at Hayley, a grin on his face, and the twinkle in his eyes had turned to a blaze. "Hayley, this could be a book from medieval times!" His voice, though still soft, was now charged with a quiet excitement, and she realized that, when he was talking about his passion, his students likely wouldn't have any trouble staying awake.

"Medieval?" She looked at him for a moment with her mouth open. "I knew it was old, but . . ."

"Where did you get this?"

"It was my father's. He died a couple of years ago."

"Oh, I am sorry."

"I didn't know him, but thank you." She looked back down at the book. "So, you can't tell what the cover says?"

"I am afraid I can not."

"Can we see what's inside?" Hayley asked.

"That is exactly what I was thinking," he smiled. "We could take it into the archive room. The lighting, temperature and humidity are carefully controlled there."

"Okay," Hayley nodded.

"That is no guarantee," Max stressed. "If this truly is an eight-hundred-year-old book, it could still disintegrate into a pile of dust." Hayley winced at that. "On the other hand, it could turn out to just be a collection of *Der Spiegel* that somebody bound in an old leather cover."

"Really? Those are the only two possibilities?"

"Well, no." He smiled again, looking back down at the book. "It could also turn out to actually be the real thing, a first edition original printing of a medieval book that could make you world famous and insanely wealthy."

"But not if it's a pile of dust."

"That is correct."

Hayley looked from Max to the book and back again, struggling.

"I'd love to know what it is," she finally said.

Max grinned conspiratorially as he stood up.

"Come with me." He picked up the Lucite box from his desk and Hayley followed him out the door.

§

Hayley remembered the scene in the movie *Angels & Demons*, where Tom Hanks visited the Vatican Archive. Stotzheim University's archival reading room, she discovered, wasn't anywhere near that state-of-the-art but, according to Max, it was kept at a relatively constant 40% humidity and a temperature of 20°.

"Twenty degrees?" Hayley asked. "What is that in American?"

"I am not sure," Max smiled.

Hayley decided that, while it was cool, it wasn't intolerable, perhaps just a little cooler than 70° Fahrenheit, not much different than the wine cellar where the book had been stored. They chose a table in the corner, where they could talk quietly without disturbing anybody else, though at the moment, nobody else was there. She watched as he got a couple of foam wedges and placed them on each side of the box. He flipped the two metal clasps on the side, then he looked at Hayley.

"Are you certain?" he asked. She hesitated, then nodded. Max lifted off the top of the box and laid it aside.

"Wait," Hayley said, "shouldn't you be wearing white cotton gloves?"

"That is something of a myth," he replied. "The cotton gloves can actually do more harm than good. Handling the pages as little as possible, with clean hands, is the best."

He carefully lifted the book out of the base that had been made to fit it exactly, and he moved the base to the side along with the top. He slid the foam wedges closer together so they formed a squat V-shape that the book could lie comfortably between, both covers supported by a wedge. He placed the spine down on the table between them, and gingerly opened the front cover, listening for cracking. Satisfied, he allowed the front and back covers to rest on the supporting foam wedges, and he turned the page.

"It seems to be good quality rag paper," he said as he carefully turned another. "It is still in good condition."

Hayley leaned in close to get a look. The pages were densely covered with old gothic text, the ink a dark brownish black.

"Can you read it?" Hayley asked.

"I can," Max replied.

Hayley glanced at the clock on the wall, wondering how much time they had left.

"Don't you have a class?" she asked.

Max looked at his watch, then pulled out his phone.

"I will have my assistant take it today."

Chapter 5

His sword felt like lead in his hand. He stumbled back, almost tripping over a body lying behind him. The field was littered with them. He regained his balance and looked down at the Dane that he had just struck down.

As he watched the man die in the red mud at his feet, he tried to catch his breath. The battle had been raging for hours and, while he had lost count of how many Danes he had killed in that time, he knew that many of his countrymen had fallen as well. During those hours, the ground had become sodden with blood, which only made fighting more difficult, the sticky mud sucking at his feet with each step.

This latest incursion of Danes into northern Germany had drawn soldiers to the front near a little village called Weißesdorf, and it was disconcerting to see how close the village was now. The Danes had been pushing hard, and despite his valiant efforts, and those of his countrymen, they were losing ground.

He hunched his right shoulder, trying to ease the ache, and as he tilted his head, he felt the cut on the back of his neck open up. During the fight, the Dane's sword had bounced painfully off of the mail on his back. There was still enough force behind the swing, though, that the edge had come back down on his neck, opening a gash that now oozed fresh blood down over his shoulder blade.

As the clanging of swords continued around him, but more distant now, he scanned the battlefield. Looking past all the scattered bodies, he locked eyes with another Dane who was not engaged in a fight. Just a few feet behind him were the nearest houses of the village. He heaved a great sigh and began slogging through the bloody mud toward the Dane.

It gave him some satisfaction to see that the Dane seemed equally exhausted.

But as they came together, they each mustered the strength to swing their swords, and his arm ached anew at the clash of their blades coming together. But he had more strength left, more stamina. The power of his strikes forced the Dane backward, *causing him to trip over a body. He raised his sword and delivered the final blow.*

His peripheral vision caught the sight of a helmet moving just inches away on his right, and he instinctively swung his sword as he turned. The image that appeared in front of him tore at his heart. A child of six or seven years old had donned an old helmet, perhaps his father's, and had apparently escaped the safety of his mother and shelter to watch the battle. As the boy was standing on a fallen tree for a better vantage point, the warrior had mistaken him for an enemy and slashed him across the belly.

The little boy fell backwards onto the ground, and the warrior quickly stepped over the tree toward him. The old, discarded helmet the child wore had no faceplate, and the surprise and shock of the attack was plainly visible on his face, as were the tears slipping down into the helmet. The warrior watched helplessly as the blood pouring from the little boy's belly stopped, the little chest went still, and the eyes froze in their focus somewhere beyond him.

He felt bile rising in his throat and tears flooding his eyes as he contemplated the evil he had just done. It was not until the last moment that he saw another Dane riding toward him from the left, swinging a battle flail. When he sensed the movement, Cort turned, just as the spiked ball crashed into the side of his helmet.

The last sensation he remembered before sinking into unconsciousness was not the pain. Nor was it disappointment at having lost the battle. Instead, he felt annoyance at the pungent stink of the mud saturated with blood, now oozing into his helmet, and anguish at the knowledge that the blood of the child he had killed was now part of it.

§

Cort Rottweill awoke feeling no pain. Lying on his feather bed, he was dry and comfortable. The room, though, was strangely quiet.

He rolled over on his side, pushing his hair back on the pillow, out of his face. He spent a few seconds looking around the room. It was dark, but he could just make out some details. The cottage was small, a single room, with the bed on this side, a table and two chairs on the opposite side, and a small kitchen area in the corner. The front half of the cottage was a carpentry shop where, he now remembered, he spent most of his time, if not outside.

As was usually the case, emerging from the dream of his last battle, he felt disoriented. He still remembered all the sensations very clearly. All the sounds. All the smells. All the pain. But his wounds had healed long ago.

Most of them.

Cort sat up at the side of his bed. He felt the back of his neck, tracing the raised scar where the Dane's sword had cut him. Of course it was only a scar. But the dream was always so vivid, he had to check every time.

The memory of the dying child's face, though, had never gone away.

Cort sighed, rubbing his face. He stood up and stretched. He was only twenty-five years old, but they had been hard years. It felt like a lot more.

He was eight years old when both of his parents died from the consumption. Cort and his younger sister, Gerta, were taken in by their father's brother, but neither he nor his wife wanted them. They were poor and resented having two new mouths to feed, besides their own three children.

He and Gerta were inseparable, constant companions, until she got sick one cold winter. Their uncle and aunt refused to send for a physician, so finally Cort set off to fetch him by himself. By the time they returned through the snow and bitter cold, Gerta had died.

Cort was large, bigger than other boys his age. He was fifteen years old, and taller than his uncle. Early one morning, tired of the resentment of his uncle and aunt, and now deprived of the companionship of the one person he loved, he slipped away never to return.

He had wandered from town to town, doing odd jobs, mostly relying on his physical prowess. Sometimes it involved removing large stones from farmers' fields, or working as a laborer for carpenters.

Within a year, a substantial and powerful man of only sixteen years of age, Cort joined the army. In eight years, he fought many battles, suffered many wounds. But he gained distinction among his peers and his commanders as a mighty warrior and a fierce champion.

He had saved many of his countrymen during the last battle he fought against Denmark. It was a long and grueling battle, and many of Cort's friends were killed that day.

Cort had thought that he had been, too.

He had been found on the battlefield and his wounds tended to. His helmet had saved his life, but the crushing blow with the flail had done quite a lot of damage. When he regained consciousness, all was silent.

Now completely deaf, he received a commendation for valor on the battlefield, then he was relieved of duty. Remembering the child he had accidentally killed, he thought, as always, that the commendation was unwarranted.

Cort sleepily went to his corner kitchen and stirred the embers in the fireplace. The kindling that he added ignited and he soon had a fire going. With the first glow of dawn starting to spill through his small window, he began his day.

He did not hear the faint scratching sound outside his door.

Chapter 6

"It's strange," Hayley said, "it reads like a novel." She sat back in her chair and pondered. "I didn't realize fictional stories went back that far."

"That far?"

"That long ago."

"Oh, yes," Max said. "One of the earliest novels, some say *the* first novel, was a Japanese story called *The Tale of Genji* from the early eleventh century. But there are fictional works even older than that, as well. In fact, some would say *The Bible* is one of the oldest."

"Huh. But it sounds so modern. This book, I mean. Not *The Bible*."

"Well, I admit that I am not doing an exact translation of the text. Middle Low German would, I think, sound very strange if translated directly to English. So, I translate the thoughts rather than the words. I am paraphrasing," he smiled, "but I am being careful to do so accurately."

"Are you sure it's as old as you said?" Hayley asked, looking a little askance at him.

"You're doubting me?" he asked, donning an offended expression. He couldn't hold it for very long, though, and he ended up smiling. "Actually, I never ventured an estimate of how old the book is. Only on the language it is written in. Middle Low German was the common language in this area from, roughly, the thirteenth to the seventeenth centuries."

"So you're telling me it could only be four hundred years old?" Hayley chided.

"I am afraid that could be the case," Max smiled.

"Still medieval, though," she said.

"Yes," he chuckled.

"What about carbon dating?" Hayley asked.

"That is a definite possibility. The science department has acquired an accelerator mass spectrometer, which could possibly pinpoint its age. As I understand it, compared with older carbon dating methods, it is very fast and very accurate, within about 1%."

"Cool! What do you need to do the test?"

Max got out his phone and picked a number from his contacts. Speaking in German, he asked a couple of questions, listened to the answers, then hung up.

"They happen to be free now, so if I go there right away, they can have the result in a half hour. I just need a very small sample, like a sliver of the edge of a page. The results will be even more accurate if they have two samples."

Hayley looked at Max for a moment, as if she were weighing the pros and cons.

"Okay," she said, "I know you care at least as much about that book as I do, so I'm betting you wouldn't do anything that would damage it."

The horrified look on his face told her all she needed to know, even before she heard his answer.

"Oh, no. The size of the necessary samples will be very small, and would likely not even be noticeable."

"Alright, let's go for it," Hayley decided.

Max nodded. He stood up and went to the librarian's counter near the door and came back with a pair of scissors and a piece of scrap paper. He folded the scrap paper and set it aside. He lifted a page of the book and cut off a tiny sliver from the upper edge, then placed it in the folded scrap paper.

Then, he moved all the pages forward and carefully picked up the corner of the back end sheet. He slipped the tip of the scissors under it and snipped off a small piece of the leather cover, where it accordion-folded around the corner. He placed that sample in the folded scrap paper, as well.

They were both so focused on what he was doing, neither of them noticed that someone had entered the reading room.

"Professor Schiller," he said. Max looked up at him. The young man had dark hair, and eyes to match, but his eyes twinkled when he smiled at both of them.

"Oh, Peter," Max said as he stood up. "Is the class over already?"

Peter seemed surprised to be spoken to in English, but he responded in perfect, American English himself.

"Yes, it is. I just wanted to let you know that there were a couple of really good questions that you might want to address in your next class." He handed Max a sheet of paper, and Max looked it over briefly and nodded.

"Ah, yes, very good. Thank you." Then, he turned and looked down at Hayley. "Hayley, this is my assistant, Peter Clarkson. Peter, Hayley Hoffmann. I'm sorry, Peter, but I have to leave for a few minutes."

"Not a problem," Peter replied. "I'll just regale Ms. Hoffmann with ribald tales of the provocative and rip-roaring life of a history professor."

"Ugh," Max grunted, and he shook his head as he looked down at Hayley. "I shall return as soon as I can."

"Okay," she smiled at him. "Thank you."

"Where are you from?" Peter asked after Max left the room.

"Denver. And you?"

"Philadelphia. I'm working on my doctorate in history, particularly German history."

"Why are you so interested in German history?" Hayley asked.

"I was just always fascinated by all the Pennsylvania Dutch back home. They're so intent on staying completely separate from the rest of the world around them, holding tightly to their traditions and general way of life. While I'm not religious, I always admired their determination.

"My curiosity about them led me to look into their history, and I found that they first started coming to America all the way back in the 1600s. From there, I was curious about what led them there in the first place. My curiosity gradually grew into something of an obsession, and I became fascinated with German history in general.

"What about you? Are you a student here?"

"No, I just came out here a couple of days ago, after I learned that my father died. He lived here in Germany for almost my entire life, so I didn't know him, but apparently I inherited some of his stuff."

"Is this one of the things you inherited?" he asked, pointing to the book.

"Yes, according to Professor Schiller, it's apparently medieval."

"Wow!" Peter leaned over and looked at the page that it was open to. He looked at Hayley. "Do you mind if I read some of it?"

"I don't mind as long as you read it out loud."

Peter smiled and sat down in the chair and began reading.

Chapter 7

She pulled her legs up against her body to conserve heat. It was not freezing outside, but she was ill-clothed, and damp from the early morning dew. The stone and timbers of the cottage were not comfortable, but she hardly noticed, considering the other discomforts afflicting her.

She barely remembered how she had gotten here. She had a vague recollection of stumbling barefoot through the woods, until she no longer had the strength. Then she crawled.

She had no idea when she left yesterday afternoon of the events that would change her life. Dear God, was it only yesterday?

§

It had started out as a beautiful day. Narrow shafts of sunlight that found their way through the foliage of the ancient oak trees deposited golden freckles on the forest floor. The air was warm and carried the refrains of all manner of birds, as well as the gentle soughing of the meandering Weser River, to the ears of the young woman dressed in white.

These were Elysande's favorite moments of the day, when she could go out into the forest by herself. She enjoyed gathering herbs, but mostly, she liked to have some time to herself. The sisters were not intrusive by any means, but their presence seemed to be a constant reminder of the guilt that still sometimes plagued her.

Elysande's troublesome life had begun twenty-two years earlier, in 1262. She had been born to a prostitute and, being an inconvenience to her mother, and a hindrance to her work, was immediately sold. But life in Germany, as in most of Europe, was hard for common folk, and her new owner was no exception.

When Elysande was old enough to work, she became little more than a slave. She changed hands every few years, but despite her hard life, she blossomed into a very pretty girl. Almost inevitably, given the character of the people who traded her, when she reached her teens, her duties came to include those of a more carnal nature.

One day, when she was seventeen, she saw an opportunity and bolted. With no means to support herself, though, she eventually saw no other choice but to take up the life of a prostitute.

Elysande plied her trade near one of the gates of the town of Hameln. The walls of the convent were within sight, but while her eyes were sometimes drawn guiltily towards it, she usually forced herself to face the other direction.

Eventually, though, the guilt won out.

The sisters welcomed her, at first keeping a stern eye on her. After a time, when she had proven her commitment, she enrolled in the Magdalens, donning the white habit of their order.

That was nearly three years ago. The feelings of guilt were not nearly as bad, or as frequent, as when she first found her way here. But they still surfaced occasionally.

Admittedly, she did have an apparent tendency towards rebelliousness. Elysande was outspoken and did not hesitate to speak out when she thought that something was not right or fair. While she did not see that as a problem, apparently the nuns did. She often had to endure a scolding after boldly speaking her mind.

She wished that she could live a normal life. Get married, bear children, have a home of her own. It didn't seem like too much to ask, but apparently it was out of her reach. That opportunity just was not presenting itself.

Elysande was beginning to think that perhaps the convent was not the life for her after all, and in fact she was considering leaving the order, if she could only figure out how to support herself in a more respectable way.

That was a large part of her reason for liking her time alone. She could not get herself in trouble with the sisters when she was not with them. She could, for a while, imagine herself as the author of her own life, see herself as her own master.

Elysande's time alone, though, did not include time spent in town. She still felt a certain anxiety at the possibility of seeing a former patron. So when she left the convent, it was only to go into the forest, to gather herbs and berries for food or for medicinal preparations.

She remembered seeing a generous patch of coltsfoot in the woods a few days before. As Sister Mary Millicent had developed a bad cough, Elysande volunteered to go into the forest and gather some for a remedy.

"Ah, there it is," she said to herself as she saw the little clusters of yellow sunbursts hugging the ground ahead of her. She started gathering the plants and placing them in the basket that she always brought with her.

She was startled when hands grabbed her roughly from behind and pulled her up.

"See, men, I told you she was a nun," said the man holding her. She struggled to free herself but the man only held tighter. He turned her around and, besides her captor, she saw three other men with him.

She recognized all four of them. They had been patrons in her previous life outside the convent.

Elysande took a deep breath and started to scream, but her captor struck a savage blow to the side of her face. The breath quietly escaped her lungs as she sank to the ground into oblivion.

She didn't know for certain how long she had been unconscious. Judging by the angle of the sunlight through the foliage, she thought that perhaps as much as an hour had passed. She looked around and noticed that she did not recognize this area of the forest. They had moved her.

"Where are we?" Elysande asked, gingerly rubbing the bruise on her face.

"Don't worry about that, miss," said one of the men, the one who had grabbed her. He sneered at her. "We've come to partake of your services."

"I'm not in that business anymore," she said coldly, though it was tinged with apprehension based on her position on the ground in front of them.

"Well, that's alright. We weren't going to pay, anyway," he laughed.

47

Elysande tried to get up, but the man nodded to his companions. Two of them moved toward her and held her down, one on each side of her.

The fourth man seemed nervous.

"Hans," he said, "I don't think we should do this."

"You can go, Ansell," Hans replied casually. "But you'll miss out on this sweet morsel."

"But she's a nun," Ansell protested.

Hans ignored him. He was inching closer to Elysande and lifted the skirt of her habit, causing her to start screaming.

"There's no one around, miss," he said ominously. "Don't think anyone will hear you and come to your rescue. But since all that noise you're making will most likely interfere with our enjoyment, we will not hesitate to cut you."

Elysande now saw the knife in his hand, and she could tell by the cold and determined expression on his face that he would make good on his threat. Hans ripped her undertunic apart and began undoing his codpiece. Elysande struggled, but the two men at her sides simply held her tighter.

"Hans," Ansell said, "aren't you afraid of God's punishment for this?"

"God has to catch me first," Hans growled.

He pulled down his drawers and inched toward the struggling young woman, as the two men held her tighter.

Chapter 8

"Oh my god," Hayley said quietly. She felt shaken and horrified by Elysande's story.

It didn't have that effect on her initially. When Peter first started reading, he translated word-for-word into English, and as Max had said, it was difficult to understand. Hayley could get the general meaning, but none of the feeling being expressed.

Peter recognized the problem right away and began, as Max had called it, translating the thoughts rather than the words. He wasn't able to do it as quickly as Max did, but still, Hayley felt herself being pulled into the story.

Peter sat back and looked at Hayley with his eyebrows raised. He sighed and shook his head.

"They were definitely rough and lawless times, especially if somebody didn't fear repercussions from God or the Church."

"That poor girl," was all Hayley could say.

"I know." Peter sighed and leaned forward, getting ready to push himself up. "Well, I should probably get busy. Professor Schiller had some stuff he needed me to do."

"Okay, Peter. Thank you," she said, glancing down at the book.

"Absolutely!" He looked at Hayley, and he spoke hesitantly, almost shyly. "Are you going to be around for a while? Maybe I can show you around Hannover."

The question surprised Hayley, but she found herself considering the offer.

"Yeah," she answered, "I think I might like that."

Peter smiled and reached for a piece of scrap paper and a pencil from the box on the table.

"Here's my phone number. Give me a call."

"I will," she smiled back. "Thank you." As he stood up, Hayley looked back down at the book, and all the emotion that she had just experienced, her empathetic feelings for Elysande came rushing back. The door opened as Max came back in. He saw her face and was immediately concerned.

"What is wrong?" he asked.

"Oh, Max," she said, "Peter just read the second chapter." She saw a look that she couldn't quite identify pass across his face as he looked at Peter. Then, she saw the paper in Max's hand. "Did you get the results already?"

"I did," he nodded. "They said that there is a 98.55% likelihood that the book is at least seven hundred years old."

"Wow," Hayley whispered.

"That is so cool!" Peter added. "Well listen, I'll get out of here now. I've got stuff to do. As you know," he added, smiling at Max.

"Yes," Max replied. "Thank you."

Peter tossed a wave and a smile toward Hayley and sailed out the door.

Max sat back down in his chair.

"When's your next class?" Hayley asked.

"I have a couple of hours," he replied, glancing at the clock. "Do you want to continue with this?"

"Sure," she replied enthusiastically, "if you want to." Then, she smiled at him. "You have a little catching up to do."

"Yes," Max said, and Hayley thought she saw that elusive look again. Max skimmed the second chapter, then began reading aloud again with the next couple of chapters.

Chapter 9

delaide Schüller put her head back, shook her hair out of her eyes and sighed. She picked up the plates of food and placed them on the table, one in front of her husband Hermann.

"Thank you," he said as he picked up his spoon. The dim candle sitting in front of them sputtered momentarily from his breath. Adelaide smiled in response and sat down at her place.

"You've been very quiet this morning," she observed.

"I'm just nervous," he said. "Our crops are growing and seem healthy, but I'm afraid to be too confident. I just hope nothing changes."

Adelaide nodded slightly, all too aware of the problems they had in the past.

"Maybe you could cast a spell on the field," the young man added. Adelaide glanced at him from the corner of her eye.

"You know I don't do that," she said, but she allowed a bit of a smile, thinking happily that she had gotten over it.

"Yes, I know, my love. But perhaps now would be the time to make an exception and follow your mother's example." She shook her head but said nothing more.

She glanced at the crib, still standing lonely in the corner of their cottage, unused except for holding the clothing draped across it, and her smile dimmed. Perhaps she had not gotten over it after all.

She heard Hermann's sharp intake of breath and she looked up at him with a tear forming in her eye.

"I'm sorry, Addie," Hermann said as soon as he realized. "That was very stupid." He placed his hand softly on top of hers. Adelaide looked at him and nodded.

The Schüllers had always been poor, but their real problems had started last year, with her mother.

Rosamund had paid them a long visit early in the year, when Adelaide was pregnant. Rumors had been circulating for a while about her mother, but nobody in their circle of friends really paid any attention to them.

Even when she was a young girl, Adelaide had always known that her mother was different. But it was not until she visited them that Rosamund had begun coaxing her daughter to try her hand at casting spells.

Though Adelaide resisted at first, she was admittedly curious. In time, her curiosity won out, and she allowed her mother to teach her a few simple spells.

She found that she had a certain facility with it, and even though she felt some guilt while learning and working the spells, she pushed it aside. Within a week or so, she began experimenting with more complex charms and incantations.

When she experienced a miscarriage during one of the lessons, she was certain that it was because God was punishing her. Racked with pain and grief, and insurmountable guilt, she never made the attempt again. Hermann forgave Adelaide, but she refused to forgive herself. Now, several months later, the memory of her short time practicing witchcraft still produced a pang of conscience and a stab of guilt.

With the death of the child, the locals finally heeded the reports. They dragged Rosamund to the town square and burned her at the stake.

Adelaide narrowly escaped that fate herself when close friends and neighbors testified in her behalf.

Adelaide poked at the food in front of her, but no longer had an appetite. Her mind was elsewhere. She stood and picked up her plate from the table, while Hermann guiltily finished his breakfast.

He looked up at his wife. Her back was to him, her head down, her back hunched as she leaned against the work table. Hermann stood and went to her, placing his hand gently on the curve of her back.

Adelaide looked up at him, her eyes swimming in tears, and Hermann wrapped his arms around her.

"I'm sorry, Addie. I'm such an idiot!"

She shook her head and smiled at him, the tears flowing in rivulets down her cheeks. She buried her face in his neck and held him tightly.

§

After he finished his breakfast, Cort sighed and stood up. He leisurely cleaned up his little kitchen, then he turned to get busy with the furniture project he was currently working on.

Reynold Baron von Hoffmann, a wealthy man living in a fine fortress of a house on a hill just outside of town, had hired him to build chairs and a table for his large dining room. Cort had felled an oak tree and had finished transporting the cut sections to the small courtyard in front of his cottage. He was ready now to start preparing the timber.

When he opened his door, he nearly tripped over a battered and bruised woman lying in a heap at his threshold. She was wearing only a torn undertunic, and she wearily looked up at him. Her face was swollen and purple from the beating she had received, dried blood caked below her nose and her split lip.

Cort knelt beside her, afraid to touch her for fear of hurting her further. He gently slipped his hands under her shoulders and her knees to pick her up, and though she grimaced in pain, she did not cry out. Cort lifted her easily and carried her into his cottage, placing her on his bed.

The poor creature looked up at him between puffy, discolored eyelids, and his heart went out to her.

"I'll go get the doctor, miss," he said quietly, but he hesitated when the woman shook her head.

"I have no broken bones," she said weakly. "Only some cuts and bruises. I will be alright." Watching her face, Cort struggled to understand what she was saying. Her lips were so swollen that he could only comprehend a few words, but he understood the essence of what she said.

He went to his kitchen and dipped some water from his bucket into a bowl, and found a clean cloth to bathe her wounds.

Chapter 10

Twelve-year-old Bergh von Hoffmann hobbled down the stone staircase, expertly using his crutches as he had for most of his life. Bergh and his mother had shared an illness that, unfortunately, left her dead and left both of his legs weak and withered. But that was when he was just a baby. He had never known anything else. He learned to use crutches as he learned to walk.

Besides this infirmity, though, he had never wanted for anything of a material nature. His father owned most of the farmland and orchards around the town of Hameln, and much of the real estate inside the city walls, and in his short life, Bergh had always known luxury.

But the boy had few friends. Playing the games of the other boys was impossible to do on crutches. And it didn't help that his father was the employer and landlord of most of the people in the area. Bergh had little in common with the other children.

He struggled for just a moment with the large, heavy front door, closing it behind him, and scuffed down the wide steps. Nobody said anything to him as he left. His father was away on some kind of business, and the servants seldom paid Bergh any attention. Again, it was all he had ever known.

It took a few minutes of swinging along on his crutches to reach the wall of the town. But Bergh didn't go in the gate. He turned and followed a path that led through the forest and among scattered cottages and fields outside the wall. Cort's cottage was one of the last he came to, near the river.

Bergh had met Cort about a year before, and even though the former warrior was a formidable figure, he seemed to like Bergh. The fact that Cort actually deigned to talk to the boy made him different from other adults. Their infirmities made them feel akin, and each of them looked out for the other.

It was Bergh who told his father about Cort when von Hoffmann wanted a new table and chairs made for the dining room. Bergh knew that Cort was a very talented woodworker, and after seeing examples of his work, von Hoffmann agreed.

There was nobody in the courtyard of Cort's cottage, and Bergh was surprised. He thought that Cort would be working by now. He opened the door, knowing that Cort would not hear him knocking. Bergh was even more surprised to see a bruised and battered woman in Cort's bed.

The woman was not moving and seemed to be unconscious. The open door cast a glow of morning light across the bed and onto the far wall of the cottage, and Cort turned. His concerned expression softened with a smile when he saw Bergh.

Cort ducked through the doorway and out into the courtyard, securing the door after him. He and Bergh sat down on two little stools, crowded now among all the oak that Cort had recently hauled in for the table and chairs.

"Who's that?" Bergh asked when Cort could see his mouth.

"I don't know. She appeared at my door this morning."

"So, you don't know what happened to her?"

Cort shook his head. "Somebody beat her very badly, but more than that, I don't know." When he was cleaning her wounds, after she had passed out, he noticed evidence of rape, but he decided not to mention that to the boy. "She has been asleep for a couple of hours now."

Suddenly, something soared over the wall and fell into the courtyard. It bounced off a stack of wood, rolled a couple of times and stopped at their feet. Bergh jumped as he saw that it was a dead rat, and he heard some people, likely local boys, laughing as they ran away. Cort calmly picked up the little corpse by the tail and dropped it in his trash pile. He sat back down as if nothing had happened.

"Why doesn't that bother you?" Bergh asked when Cort looked back at him.

"What? A dead rat?"

"Not just a dead rat. All the tricks they play on you." The boy was feeling defensive for his friend, and the pitch of his voice rose with his agitation. "So many people here treat you like shit."

"You shouldn't talk like that," Cort reprimanded.

"But it's true! They play tricks on you and make fun of you every day. And you just take it from them."

"It's just because I'm deaf. Some people are superstitious. Most of them don't even know me, so I don't take it personally."

"I could never do that. If I was built like you and somebody treated me badly, I'd hurt them!"

"What good would that do?" Cort asked calmly. "It wouldn't make them like you."

"I know," Bergh said, feeling his anger slowly dissipating. "But it would make me feel better."

Cort smiled and sat back against the outer wall of his cottage. The sun felt good on his face, but there was a light, pleasant breeze shimmering through the foliage of the nearby forest.

They sat quietly for a few moments, until the door opened and the young woman slowly emerged with a blanket wrapped around her. Cort quickly stood up and offered the stool to her. She eased herself down onto the stool and smiled at him, though it looked more like a grimace. The swelling had gone down a bit, but her mouth was still stiff and sore.

"Thank you for helping me," she said. To fend off the pain, she tried to move her mouth as little as possible when she talked. Cort again missed part of what she said, so he looked at Bergh, who repeated it for him.

"You're welcome," Cort said. In response to the puzzled expression on her face, he explained, "I'm deaf. I must see your lips to know what you are saying." She gently felt her pained lips and understood the problem.

"My name is Elysande," she said.

"I am Cort Rottweill," he motioned toward Bergh, "and this is my friend, Bergh von Hoffmann." Elysande nodded weakly toward them. "Are you hungry?" Cort asked.

Elysande closed her eyes and put her head back against the wall as Cort had just minutes ago. "No, thank you." A few moments passed and Cort thought that she had fallen asleep. But then she opened her eyes and looked at him. "Herr Rottweill, please don't let me keep you from whatever you need to do."

Cort glanced at Bergh and, knowing that he needed to work on the von Hoffmann table and chairs, he decided to get started on preparing the wood for the project.

Chapter 11

"Is Hoffmann a common name in Germany?" Hayley asked, her eyebrows bunched together.

"Yes," Max replied. "Perhaps not like Smith or Jones in America, but it is pretty common."

"Huh," Hayley replied. The first time she had heard von Hoffmann's name mentioned, it had caught her ear. Could it have been merely a coincidence that a book with characters named Hoffmann would have been owned by someone named Hoffmann? Based on Max's answer, though, it could be quite likely.

"Well," Max said, "I am afraid it is time for me to leave. I have a class in a few minutes."

"Of course, Max," Hayley said.

Max carefully closed the book and eased it into the base of the Lucite box. Then, he looked at her.

"Feel free to say no," he said, "but if you like, I could hold on to the book and translate the chapters for you, including the ones we have already read. Then, not only would you have the book, but you would have a translation of what it says."

Hayley pondered for a while. She had been so intrigued by the book when she found it, and now that she was finding out what it said, she was even more curious. She hardly knew Max, but as a dedicated history professor, she knew he would take care of it. In what little time she had spent with him, the opinion she had formed of him had been a good one. And it *would* be nice to have a written translation of the book.

"How long do you think it would take?"

Max glanced at the book and did a quick estimate.

"A few days. Maybe a week, or two at the most. Perhaps we could get together again in a couple of days, and I could give you what I have completed by then. And every day or two after that, I could add to it for you. That way you would not have to wait until I am completely finished to be able to read it."

"Okay," Hayley finally replied. "I think I'll take you up on your offer."

Max smiled and nodded, and he slipped the top onto the box, snapping the clasps closed. He reached into the pocket of his jacket and pulled out a business card.

"Call me if you have any questions," he said, handing her the card, "or if you want the book back, or . . ." he paused a little nervously. Then, he looked up at her face. "Or anything else."

"I will," Hayley said. "Thank you, Max."

Max smiled and started to stand up, the Lucite box in his hands. Hayley looked apprehensively at the book.

"Uh, do you have someplace safe to keep that?"

"I do," he replied. "It will be locked in my office. Then, I will take it home with me. I have a room at my house which is like this, with the lighting, temperature and humidity carefully controlled."

"Okay," Hayley replied, perhaps a little less anxious.

"Do not worry, Hayley Hoffmann. I will take good care of this for you."

§

After interacting with several people on the campus, and spending one-on-one time with both Max and Peter, Hayley felt a little lonely as she ate her lunch by herself at the house. But she decided that it was as good a time as any to start going through some of the things in storage in the attic and the basement.

She discovered that there was a rather nice stereo system, with speakers throughout the house. Her father had apparently loved music as much as she did. There was a large collection of vinyl records and CDs, and she selected a classic Dave Brubeck CD. As *Blue Rondo à la Turk* began, she cranked up the volume and the frantic piano in 9/8 time filled the house.

Forty minutes later, as *Pick Up Sticks* ended, Hayley had four boxes placed near the stairs in the attic that she had already determined were destined for the trash. There were two boxes to donate (she would have to ask someone's recommendation for a good charity in Hannover), and five boxes that she set aside to spend more time going through.

Those last five boxes, based partly on the way they were packed, contained things that seemed like items that her father had placed more value on. Hayley had spent almost all of *Take Five* looking at a photo album in one of those boxes, trying to get a sense of who her father was, and what his life had been like. Finally, she decided to put it aside for later.

The next album was John Coltrane's *Giant Steps*. By the time it was finished, she had added two more boxes to the trash category, one to donate, and four more for spending more time with.

As she looked at those nine boxes of her father's things that she had put aside to spend more time with, she suddenly felt sad. What must his life have been like? From her mother, she knew, to an extent, what it had been like in America, and based on what Elsbeth said, that pattern had continued here in Germany. Looking around, it seemed that he obviously experienced a certain amount of success at his unethical lifestyle. But in the end, his life amounted to a house and a bunch of boxes of stuff that a daughter he never knew was going through to decide whether to keep or not.

She decided that she didn't want to spend the evening alone in this house. A night on the town sounded good to her, and she remembered Peter's invitation. She went downstairs and found his phone number and called him.

"Hello?" he answered, not recognizing the number displayed.

"Hi, Peter, it's Hayley."

"Oh, hi!" he replied enthusiastically.

"So," Hayley said, "when you offered to show me the town, was this evening a possibility?"

"Absolutely! What are you up for?"

"Well, nothing too crazy. Maybe dinner and a few of the sights."

"We can do that. What part of town are you in?"

"I'm on Garbsener Landstraße. About fifteen minutes northwest of the university."

Peter named a few restaurants, Italian, Mediterranean, Greek, but Hayley wanted to know more about German cuisine, so they decided on a local café a couple of miles from her house.

"How about I meet you there at 6:00?" Hayley suggested.

"I'll be there."

§

The place was noisy, full of locals, apparently, as Hayley didn't hear a word of English, except for Peter. Looking at the menu, she asked lots of questions, and Peter patiently explained what the dishes were. Hayley ordered something called *Rinderrouladen mit Kartoffelnudeln*, a beef dish served with potato noodles.

"So, how do you like Germany so far?" Peter asked as he sipped his beer.

"I have to admit I haven't seen much of it yet," Hayley replied. "I've seen the airport, my house, the university and this place, and whatever happened to be in between. But I've seen enough to realize that my expectations were off."

"How so?"

"I guess my main point of reference involved movies set in Germany, usually around World War II. So I was picturing concrete bunkers and rows of grey block residences."

"Ah," Peter smiled. "There still are some of those, particularly, I think, in Berlin. But Germany's come a long way since the war."

"Oh, I'm sure of it. And that's not to say I don't like the old architecture. My house, for instance. It's a beautiful old place. I'm sure it was around before the war."

"What's it like?"

"It's three stories tall, mostly white, but the vertical and horizontal structure of big dark wood is exposed."

"Yeah, that's *fachwerk*, or half-timbered construction. It's very common throughout Germany."

"It's beautiful. It's like an illustration from a book of old nursery rhymes."

"It could be," Peter replied. "Some of the structures are quite old. In fact, the oldest is down near Stuttgart. It's a block of row houses built in the early thirteen-hundreds."

"Wow!"

"Yeah." Peter looked at her for a moment and smiled. "So, you like old stuff huh?"

"I do. I love antiques. My favorite art was by a guy named Alphonse Mucha, a Czech artist from the eighteen-hundreds. I love old black-and-white movies. I'm a music teacher, so I love music, but my favorite is classical; or jazz, but it has to be from the fifties or before."

"And you love old books, too," Peter pointed out.

"That's true," Hayley smiled. The waitress approached their table holding a plate in each hand. She placed them on the table in front of Peter and Hayley, and she looked at their mugs.

"*Möchtest du mehr Bier?*" she asked.

"More beer?" Peter translated. Hayley looked at her nearly empty mug and shrugged.

"Maybe one more."

"*Ja bitte. Danke.*"

The waitress nodded and left.

"So," Peter said as he cut a bite of his *Sauerbraten*, "how goes the translation?"

"I assume it's going well," Hayley replied. "Professor Schiller read a couple more chapters after you left. He offered to take the book and work on the translation in the evenings. So he's probably working on it now."

"You gave it to Professor Schiller?" Peter asked, a note of surprise in his voice. "You're very trusting."

"I don't know, he seems trustworthy."

"I suppose."

"Why?" Hayley asked, suddenly feeling apprehensive. "Is there something I should know about?"

"No, I'm sure it's fine," he said, his tone not entirely convincing. "It's just that, with something that valuable, I don't know if I could ever let it out of my sight."

"How valuable?"

"Well, obviously I couldn't put any kind of exact price on it based on the short time I saw it, and besides, I'm no expert. But medieval documents sell for a lot of money. I mean if you follow the antiquities markets, you'll find manuscripts from the Middle Ages *starting* at around ten thousand dollars and going up into the millions."

Hayley almost choked on the bite of *Rinderrouladen* she was swallowing.

"Oh my god," she whispered.

"Are you familiar with the Gutenberg Bible?"

"Yes," she said excitedly, "I just thought of that yesterday when I first found the book. I saw the one at the New York Public Library a few years ago."

The waitress came back and left two full mugs of beer and took their empty ones.

"Yeah," Peter continued, "and that one in New York is not even a complete one. There are nearly fifty copies of the Gutenberg around the world, whereas I think it may be safe to say that your book is one of a kind. A complete Gutenberg Bible is estimated to be worth, today," he paused for effect, "twenty-five to thirty-five million dollars. Individual pages sell for fifty to a hundred-and-fifty thousand!"

"Damn!" Hayley said. Then, she giggled. "Just think, if you tore out all the pages and sold them separately for that much, you could get even more!"

Peter snickered, his dark eyes twinkling.

"You know, I think it's going to be very warm where you're going."

"I'll be sure to take some shorts." She giggled again as she picked up her mug. "It doesn't take much alcohol to make me loopy."

Peter smiled as he picked up his mug and held it up for a toast.

"To your new-found wealth, and may it never go to your head like the beer is doing." Hayley grinned, and they clunked their mugs together and took a drink.

"So," Peter said, looking askance at her, "are you really as happy as you seem?"

"Happy?"

"Yeah, you look like you're almost always on the cusp of smiling, like there's always a smile waiting right below the surface."

Hayley smiled at his observation, then seemed embarrassed for smiling.

"Like that," Peter pointed out. "Even if you're not smiling yet, it doesn't take much to bring one out."

"When I was little," Hayley ruminated, "one of the things I remember about my father was him scolding me for giggling and laughing so much. I guess it got on his nerves. He was going through some hard times then, so I'm sure it wasn't *just* my laughter, but he did it enough to make me self-conscious about it.

"After he left, well, I was sad, obviously, but at the same time, I think I felt a certain amount of relief. I was finally able to be myself without worrying about whether it was going to make him angry.

"My mother has a silly side, too, and it really came out when I was growing up. I think we just encouraged each other, laughed at each other's jokes, developed our senses of humor together.

"So, I guess to answer your question, I'd have to say that I'm fairly happy. But I think there's still some of that self-consciousness there, so some of the laughter may be a cover for that."

"Hmm. Well, personally, I can't see what you could possibly have to feel self-conscious about. You're an absolute delight to be around."

"Thank you," Hayley said, her eyes suddenly glossy. They ate a few more bites in silence. Finally, Hayley sat back.

"I don't think I can do any more."

"Okay," Peter replied.

"And I don't think I can go out on the town like I wanted to," she added with some embarrassment.

"Oh?"

"I think it's the jetlag. And I'm sure the beer isn't helping. I'm just really wiped out."

"Oh, of course," Peter said sympathetically. "Yeah, that's right, you just got here yesterday morning, didn't you?" Hayley nodded. "Sure, we can call it quits when we're finished here."

"Thank you."

"I'm not sure I'm comfortable with the thought of you driving, though. I think I should drive you home."

She was about to wave it off and say that she was fine, but she realized that he had a point.

"But then one of our cars will still be here," she protested. Despite the good impression Peter had made on her so far, she almost expected him to suggest that he spend the night with her, then they could drive back to the restaurant in the morning to get her car.

"No, it's no big deal," he said. "You said your place is just a couple of miles away. I can drive you home in your car, get a taxi back here for next to nothing, and drive my car home."

"You're sure you don't mind?"

"Well, I'm not going to deny that I'm disappointed that I can't spend more time with you this evening. I was looking forward to getting to know you a little better. But no, it's not a problem at all."

"Thank you, Peter," Hayley said, smiling appreciatively. "That's very kind of you."

"Oh, don't be silly. I'm happy to do it."

Peter ate the last couple of bites of his *Sauerbraten* and washed it down with the last of his beer. He settled the bill, reluctantly accepting the money that Hayley pushed toward him, and they got up and left.

"Where's your car?" he asked when they were outside. Hayley pointed to the red BMW 507. "Sweet ride! That's not a rental, is it?"

"No, it's not. Just another old thing I inherited from my father."

"Wow."

They got in the car and Peter started it up. He smiled as he pulled out onto the street. Hayley told him where to turn, and they pulled up in front of her house in less than five minutes.

"Damn," Peter said, "now I wish your place was farther away." Hayley smiled, and Peter looked up at the house. "In other news, I think you're right. I'd say this place has been here for well over a hundred years. That is a gorgeous example of *fachwerk*."

"Yeah, it's definitely growing on me," Hayley said. She looked at Peter as she yawned. "I'm sorry about cutting the evening short."

"Oh, Hayley, don't worry about it. Really. It's a school night. I've got stuff I should be doing anyway."

"When does the term end?" she asked. "Isn't it about over now?"

"No, I'm afraid not," he smiled. "Here in Germany, the terms are a little different than they are back home. The year is divided into a *Wintersemester* and a *Sommersemester* which, even though those are both German words, are exactly what they sound like. We're currently in the early part of the *Sommersemester*."

"Huh," Hayley replied groggily.

"Okay," Peter smiled, getting out his phone, "that's my cue. I'm going to call a taxi and get out of here so you can get some rest."

He made the call quickly, then disconnected and looked at Hayley.

"Thank you, Peter," she said. "I had a good time, even if it was over sooner than expected."

"Yeah, we guys can't seem to get the hang of that." He grinned at Hayley. She looked blankly at him for a moment until his double entendre sank in. Then she sputtered in response as they got out of the car.

"I hope I can see you again," Peter laughed.

"I'd like that."

Chapter 12

Hayley woke up Tuesday morning feeling rested and refreshed. Unlike the night before, when she could barely sleep at all, she had gone to bed shortly after Peter left and slept for nine hours straight.

Feeling so rested did wonders for her motivation. After a quick breakfast, and after selecting twelve rousing CDs to play in the CD changer – classical this time – she got to work, picking up where she had left off in the attic.

There were only a few boxes left, mainly clothing items, and sorting them didn't take long. Before the Haydn trumpet concertos were finished, she had sorted the last of them.

She spent a little time on her cell phone, checking online about the trash and recycling programs in Hannover. When she pulled the car back into the garage after Peter left the night before, Hayley had seen the various colored bins, and a few minutes after her call, she knew what to do with them.

After wrestling the seven boxes of trash downstairs, she welcomed the time it took to sit and sort the papers and plastics into their respective bins. The four boxes of donations were a little trickier, since she still hadn't asked anyone about a good charity. She made a brief call to Elsbeth and had a couple of possibilities. She made a phone call to each and, finding someone who spoke English at the second one, she arranged a pickup time.

That still left a ponderous ten boxes of more personal items to go through. After spending what was left of the morning, and most of the afternoon on that, she felt emotionally exhausted. The vast majority of the items meant nothing to her. The things she kept for herself had nothing to do with any connection to her father, but just because it was cool stuff. Other things she put aside to allow Elsbeth to look at and see if she wanted.

When the twelfth CD ended, Hayley sighed and decided that she was done for the day. She poured herself a glass of the Riesling from the fridge, and she found Max's business card and dialed his number.

"*Hallo,*" he answered.

"Hi, Max, it's Hayley."

"Hayley, I am glad you called. I have a few chapters for you."

"Really? Already?"

"Yes, I am fascinated. I can not get enough of this. I even had Peter teach another one of my classes today. I want to spend all my time on this."

"You won't get in trouble for this, will you?" Hayley asked.

"No," Max laughed, "I am being responsible, even though I do not want to. Would you like to get together tomorrow? You could come to the campus . . . or perhaps I could take you to dinner? That would have the added benefit of allowing me time to get another chapter or two finished for you during the day."

"Dinner would be wonderful," she smiled. "I'm excited to see what you've got for me."

She arranged to meet him at the campus at five o'clock and they would leave from there. She thanked him in advance and disconnected. That still left almost twenty-four hours for her to fill.

Aside from the book, she hadn't even started on all the stuff in the basement, but she decided that she had done enough for today. She spent a little time preparing some of the food in the kitchen, with a lot of help from her phone. While the bratwurst and nudels cooked, she did a little more research on her phone.

She was able to pull up Netflix.de and, while she ate her dinner, she watched a couple of episodes of shows that she had been following back home, after she changed the language to English.

Watching the familiar programs, she found, was oddly comforting to her. For a while, it didn't feel as if she was five thousand miles away from anybody she knew. In the big, empty old house, she felt at home.

She cleaned up the kitchen, then went up to bed.

§

As it turned out, teaching music to elementary school students was no preparation for carrying eleven full boxes of trash and donations down two flights of stairs. Hayley woke up the next morning tired and sore. Having gotten so much accomplished the day before, she decided to take an R&R day.

She spent time wandering the grounds, reveling in the oak forest and the songs of birds. Set back from the road behind the stone wall, all she heard were the abundant sounds of nature.

She also started a subscription to an online language site, figuring that, as long as she was here, it wouldn't hurt to learn German. After a few minutes, she decided she wasn't too sure about that.

She meandered around the basement a bit, ignoring the boxes of stored items, looking curiously over the rows of wine bottles, and at the antique ship's compass and the other two books in the little room off the wine cellar. And she tried to renew her commitment to learn the language.

By the time she was ready to admit that she was bored, it was time to start getting ready to meet Max.

§

"I think you are going to be quite excited," Max said, his eyes gleaming. After meeting at the campus, Hayley agreed to go with him in his car. She decided that tousled was the natural state of his hair. She didn't mind, though, and she realized as she looked at him in his brown tweed blazer that he was a very good-looking man.

Even though it was a rather nice restaurant he took her to, Max had brought his briefcase in with him. After he helped Hayley with her order, he pulled out several pages of printed paper.

"You've gotten a lot done!" she replied, leafing through the first few chapters that had already been read to her, and she laid them aside.

"Yes," he said, "but you need to read the next chapter."

Hayley looked askance at him, wondering what the look on his face meant. She settled back in her chair and began reading.

Chapter 13

Morning sunlight streamed through the high faceted window into the large bedchamber. The grand room was furnished lavishly, with lush tapestries on the walls and plush coverings on the bed. The air was still, but a few dust particles glowed as they drifted lazily through the sharp beams of sunlight slashing through the room.

Reynold von Hoffmann lounged on the thick mattress, lying on his side, and looked at the mass of blonde hair directly in front of him. He smiled and pulled himself closer to Katarina. He placed his hand lightly on her side, caressing her softly, then he slid his hand gently down around her belly. He pulled her up tight against his body, enjoying the warmth of her naked skin against his.

Katarina squirmed, her buttocks pressing against him, and he felt a stirring in his loins. She moaned into wakefulness and turned to face him, golden strands of hair backlit by the morning sunlight.

"Good morning," she smiled at him, her eyes still half-closed.

"Yes, it certainly is, Kat." He felt her breasts pressing against his chest, and as she leaned into him to kiss him, the stirring in his loins increased. To the point that she could now feel it too.

"What do we have here?" she smiled, and she pressed harder against him. "We should do something about this."

"I wish we could, my love, but I'm afraid I have to go." He kissed her now pouting lips.

"Oh, must you?" she whined. "I'm always lonely when you're away."

"I'm sorry, but yes, I have quite a busy day today." He kissed her again, then reluctantly pulled away and got up. Katarina sat up in bed and watched him, knowing that the covers had fallen down into her lap. As he got dressed, Reynold looked at her, watching him with her breasts exposed, and he smiled.

"You know I am very strong," he said. "I can resist your temptations." She huffed and pulled the covers up. "At least for a short time," he finished, and somewhat mollified, Katarina's face softened with a slight smile.

Reynold finished arranging his clothing, then he went around to Katarina's side of the bed. He bent over and kissed her lightly. She was still sulking, but she put her arms around his neck and returned the kiss.

"I shall be with you again in a couple of days, sweetheart," Reynold said.

He gently caressed her cheek and smiled at her. Then he left.

§

Adelaide kissed her husband, feeling much better. Hermann had always been a kind, sensitive man, although he sometimes spoke without thinking. Things he said sometimes hurt her, but she knew it was unintentional, and he always tried to make it better. His remark about employing her mother's art had hurt her, but she felt better now.

"You should go," she said. Hermann was usually busy in the field by now.

"Are you sure?" he asked. "I could stay with you today if you need me to."

"No, I'll be fine."

Adelaide made a point of smiling and nodding, to show him that she was strong enough. She didn't want him to get any further behind on his work. They were already late on paying their rent.

As if to underscore that last thought, there came a sudden loud pounding on their door.

Hermann looked down at Adelaide, his brows furrowed in confusion. He went to the door and pulled it open. The early morning light streamed in over the city a short distance away, and he could see a large, muscular man standing outside, his face cold and stone-like.

"Yes?" Hermann said. "Who are you?"

"Gunter," the man said. "I work for Baron von Hoffmann. You've been ordered to vacate this property."

"What? Ordered by whom?" He looked at Adelaide as she came up behind him.

72

"By Baron von Hoffmann," he said, turning slightly to glance to his side.

Reynold Baron von Hoffmann sat, impassive and aloof, upon his horse a short distance away, watching the proceedings without emotion.

Hermann tried to think of what to do, but the ideas were not coming. Adelaide, tears in her eyes, focused her attention on Reynold. She took a deep breath, squared her shoulders and approached him, while Hermann watched curiously.

"Baron von Hoffmann," she said meekly, "please show us mercy. We have nowhere to go."

"You should have thought of that earlier, Frau Schuller," Reynold slowly said in a tone that sounded as if he was annoyed to be bothered by this. "As I told your husband a few days ago, you are two months behind on your rent. My mercy has run out."

"But our crops failed last year. We have had little to live on since then."

"You have been living here for five years," Reynold sighed, irritated to have to deal with her. "You have experienced some kind of problem with your crops three of those years. I have been patient with you. I allowed you more time to pay your rent last year after your baby died."

The tears in Adelaide's eyes tumbled down her cheeks at hearing the mention of her dead child again.

"Yes sir," she said quietly with her eyes downcast. "Thank you."

"Your neighbors," Reynold continued unmoved, motioning toward the north, "the Reinhardts, worked hard and I rewarded them by granting them ownership of their home and land. This could have been yours."

"With respect, sir," Hermann said, coming up behind his wife, "but that was many years ago, even before we came. I have not heard of you doing this at all since then."

"Yes," Reynold replied coldly. "It appears I must exercise greater care in choosing my tenants. Now if you vermin will stop stalling, please clear out your things and be on your way."

Adelaide felt the heat of anger surge through her body. Hermann, seeing her stiffen, took her arm and pulled her toward the cottage.

A few neighbors were gathering now and watched from a distance, some looking with sympathy at the Schüllers, some with disgust at Reynold. As Hermann dragged his wife through the door, her eyes paused in the corner where the crib stood. She sighed and went to it, gathering up the clothing draped across it, and as she did so, she uncovered a book.

Hermann started sadly gathering some of their larger possessions as Adelaide opened the grimoire. She was surprised to see it – she thought they had gotten rid of all of those things. She remembered the thrill she had felt when her mother first introduced her to it.

She suddenly felt empty and cold, their home taken from them on the heels of the multiple reminders of her dead child. But she didn't feel helpless.

Looking at the page that was open before her, she remembered the revulsion she had felt when she first saw this page last year. At that time, she could not imagine making use of these instructions. Now she almost relished the thought.

Hermann went outside and pulled their rickety cart around to the front of the cottage, but apparently they were not moving out quickly enough for Reynold.

"Gunter," he said with a bored tone of voice, "make them hurry up."

The big man, standing just to the side of the cart, took the crossbow hanging from his belt and pointed it threateningly at Hermann. Hermann put his hands up as if to pacify him, but at the moment, he was very close and bumped him. Gunter pushed Hermann toward the door, where he collided with Adelaide who was just coming out, knocking her down.

The whole incident took just a few seconds, but Reynold was getting impatient.

"Get these cockroaches out of there!" he growled, and Gunter struck Hermann on the back of the neck with the butt of the crossbow. Hermann fell down unconscious.

"Sorry, mein Herr," Gunter said toward Reynold.

Adelaide looked at Hermann, and saw the bump already rising on the base of his skull. She stood up and raised her eyes toward Reynold, her lip curled in anger, and she began reciting the ancient mysterious words from the book.

To Gunter and Reynold, they sounded like gibberish, but they began to experience an unmistakable sense of dread and fear as she continued.

There was a faint rustling sound from the weeds and shrubberies all around them, and Reynold's horse began nickering nervously. Adelaide continued reciting the incantation, as the wind came up.

Those watching from a distance began huddling together in groups, while some dispersed to their homes, closing their doors. Adelaide's eyes were still tightly focused on Reynold as the rustling sound was growing louder, and Reynold was finding it difficult to control his horse.

"Gunter!" he shouted, "make her stop!"

"Frau Schüller," Gunter said as he pointed his crossbow at her. Adelaide ignored him, still repeating the spell, and she suddenly raised her hands in an aggressive gesture toward Reynold. Gunter loosed the bolt from his crossbow, and it embedded itself in Adelaide's abdomen.

The force of the shot dropped her to the ground and threw her back against the door jamb, and she found herself facing Gunter. The shock interrupted her recitation, but after a moment, as shock began numbing the pain, she continued repeating the phrase.

An expression of unexplainable fear and confusion washed over Gunter's face and he hurried to try to fit another bolt to the crossbow. But he was too late.

The weeds and shrubberies around them suddenly exploded as a myriad rats swarmed toward Gunter, quickly covering his body, climbing his legs. The man screamed, flailing about in a panic, as he disappeared under a churning blur of grey and brown.

Gunter's screams became muffled. He kept pulling the rodents from his body by the handfuls, but there were always more to replace them. They were clawing and biting, and the gruesome grey and brown churning mass started turning red.

Still the rats kept coming, and the shape of Gunter was no longer recognizable. What was left of him had fallen to the ground. The only movement now was from the still-growing, agitating mountain of rats swarming over the spot where the man had been.

Adelaide knew that something had gone very wrong. She knew that she had to turn her attention back toward Reynold, but sitting on the ground now in her open doorway, she had so little strength. She could feel her energy draining away with her blood.

She turned her head a little, trying to find him. She could hear his horse snorting and squealing somewhere off to her right, but she could not see Reynold. She repeated the last phrase of the ancient incantation as, with one last burst of strength, she forced herself to turn in the direction that she had last seen Baron von Hoffmann, but she could not turn enough. As her final breath left her body, her eyes came to rest on the walls of Hameln.

§

There was little left of Gunter by the time the rats left. The bones were picked clean, and there were even scrapes on the bones where the rats had gnawed the tissues from them. The only indication that this was not an old skeleton was the quagmire of fresh blood saturating the ground beneath it.

Seeing the beginnings of the disturbance, the neighbors had disappeared long before this. Reynold Baron von Hoffmann, after seeing the rats inexplicably turn as a group and slip away in the direction of Hameln, looked one last time at the gory remains, then wheeled his horse around and rode away.

Chapter 14

"Whoa!" Hayley said, looking up at Max as she turned the page she had just finished face-down on the stack. "Oh my god, that was intense!"

"Yes, it was," Max agreed with a smile, as the waiter arrived at their table and placed their orders in front of them. Hayley reluctantly pushed the papers aside.

As they started eating, Hayley glanced at the papers again, but resisted the urge.

"You are wanting to read while you eat?" Max asked with a grin.

"No," Hayley lied. "That would be rude." She suspected, though, that he saw through her ruse. But then, she looked at the papers again. "That first part, with Katarina and Baron von Hoffmann. That seemed pretty risqué for something written in medieval times."

"It was not common," Max confirmed, "but not unheard of. Particularly if the writer did not happen to be afraid of the Church."

"Hmm, interesting. Peter said something similar, in reference to Elysande's rapists."

"Did he?"

Again, Hayley noticed that expression on his face that she couldn't figure out.

"Max, what is it?" she asked. "What is it about Peter that makes you look that way whenever I mention him?"

Max seemed momentarily surprised and embarrassed, then shook his head.

"No, it is nothing," he said, his voice even quieter than usual. "I am sorry. Peter is a nice young man. He is just – different." He shook his head again, and his face suffused with color. "Although I admit it could just be the difference in our cultures."

"Because he's American?" Hayley asked, and then a smile crept across her face. "Am I different?"

"Now you are making fun out of me." Hayley shook her head, but having just put a bite of food in her mouth, she couldn't respond immediately. Max continued, looking at her. "You *are* different, but in a good way."

Now, it was Hayley's turn to feel embarrassed, and she felt that old self-conscious feeling come over her.

"So, tell me about yourself, Max," she said abruptly in an effort to shift the subject of the conversation.

Max raised his eyebrows as he briefly thought about his answer.

"I was born and raised here in Hannover. My mother died a few years ago, as you know. My father is a lawyer like his father before him. So are my two brothers."

"Huh," Hayley mused. "How did you end up as a history professor?"

"I love history," Max replied simply with a shrug. "My family does not understand. But the past is what shaped us into who we are. How can we truly know ourselves if we do not know who we were and where we came from?"

"Wow," Hayley replied, narrowing her eyelids as she pondered, "I think that's actually pretty close to *my* philosophy, although I don't think I've ever really articulated it. But I love history, I love old things, antiques, old music. I could spend hours looking at old photo albums." Then, she looked back at Max. "You said your family doesn't understand. Do they have a problem with you being a history professor?"

He raised an eyebrow as he looked at her.

"There has been some disapproval," he replied quietly. His expression was restrained, but Hayley noticed the undercurrent of tension in his voice.

"I'm sorry," she said sympathetically. "Do you not want to talk about it?"

"There is not much to say," Max shrugged again. "My family is wealthy. Money is everything to them, and I have turned my back on the family business to pursue something that does not pay nearly as well. My father thinks I am a fool and have shamed the family."

"Oh, Max, you're doing something you love. If it pays the bills, what more could you ask for?"

"What do you do?" Max asked. Hayley wasn't sure if he asked purely out of interest, or to shift the focus off of himself.

"I'm a music teacher. I teach elementary school students."

"Do you love it?"

"I do," she replied, her face beaming in confirmation. "I love music and I love the kids. It doesn't pay much, either, but it's the perfect job for me."

Max nodded his head, and Hayley could see that he understood completely.

They sat in silence as they ate a few bites of their meal after that. Finally, Max seemed to regain a sense of enthusiasm.

"So, what do you think of the story so far?"

"It's fascinating!" Hayley replied, instantly exuberant. "I can't wait to see where it goes."

Max looked at her for a moment, and Hayley thought she saw a puzzled expression flash across his face.

"Do you not know the story?" Max asked.

"What story?"

"The story of the Pied Piper."

"The Pied Piper of Hamelin Town?" she said. "Of course!" Then, recognition flashed across her face. "Oh, in English, we know it as Hamelin, not Hameln. I didn't put it together until now."

"Ah," Max said. "I will write it as Hamelin from now on."

"So this story is the fairy tale of the Pied Piper?"

"Oh, no, it is no fairy tale," Max said, quite seriously. "It is based on a true story." Seeing the expression of disbelief on Hayley's face, he quickly elaborated. "I do not mean the story of the man with the magical flute. Historians believe that is an allegory for some other occurrence. But something really happened then that inspired this story."

"Really?"

"Yes, in the year 1284, the children of the town went missing. Some think they were lost to The Plague, others feel that, due to overpopulation of the area, many children were sent away or sold, a practice that was not uncommon at the time. There are actually several theories as to what may have happened."

"I'll bet none of those theories involved a woman conjuring rats out of thin air," Hayley said.

"No," Max smiled, "that, I think, is a new one."

"Or an old one," Hayley corrected.

"True," Max chuckled.

Chapter 15

Mayor Hildebrandt tore a chunk of pumpernickel off the small loaf sitting on the tray on his desk, spread some raspberry jam on it and slipped it in his mouth. His wife had always loved raspberry jam. When she was alive, he never cared for it as much as she did. He always felt it was too tart. But in the years since she passed away, he seemed to eat it more, enjoying it in her memory.

The morning sunlight streamed through the window, brightly illuminating the papers strewn across his desk. Looking at the mess, he stretched and yawned. The morning had not started off very well. He had been woken in the early hours by representatives of the convent about a missing Magdalen. A former prostitute, she had disappeared the previous afternoon.

While he assured them that he would institute a search, he did not expect it to be very fruitful. It was not unheard of for former prostitutes to leave the order when they found it difficult to conform to the rigid lifestyle.

After sunrise, Hildebrandt had sent out officers to carry out a search for the missing girl, and a couple of the leaders had already reported back. No success.

All of that was why he was having a late breakfast at his desk. He looked at the pumpernickel and jam again, pondering briefly, and decided instead on a slice of bratwurst and cheese. He washed it down with a swallow of beer, then looked back at the papers in front of him. Numerous things required his attention, but he was tired. It was difficult to focus on any of them.

He turned in his chair to look out the window. It was a beautiful morning, and through the wavy distortions in the glass, he saw people out going about their business in the sunshine. A few of them were running, and while Mayor Hildebrandt was mildly curious why, he decided he was just procrastinating.

He vigorously rubbed his face with his palms, trying to wake himself up. As he stopped, he heard a rustling sound nearby. He turned back toward his desk, thinking that papers might have been blowing in a draft. A movement caught his eye, and he looked at his breakfast tray. A rat was perched there, chewing a bit of pumpernickel.

"Shoo!" Hildebrandt said, waving his hand toward the rodent. The rat stopped its chewing and jerked in surprise. The rat looked warily at him, evidently startled by his movement, but apparently not affected otherwise. After a few moments, the rat resumed eating the bit of pumpernickel in its gnarled little hands.

Mayor Hildebrandt had never seen a rat so inured to the presence of humans as to just sit there and look at him. Still, though he was curious, he didn't want vermin eating his food, so he stood up from his chair. At that point, the rat, realizing that this human meant business, scurried across the desk and down to the floor, disappearing in the still dark shadows of the doorway at the back of Hildebrandt's office.

§

The sun was climbing into the sky as Reynold raced around to the back of the house, tying his horse to a post. He pounded on the door and waited impatiently for it to open. When it did, he placed a foot on the threshold, but stopped himself from going further.

"Is His Grace at home?" he asked Helga, the cook.

"No, Baron von Hoffmann," Helga replied.

"What about Her Grace, the Duchess?"

"Yes, Baron von Hoffmann, she is upstairs."

"Please send for her!" he said, as he stepped through the door. The kitchen staff was busy with preparations for the midday meal, and they made a point of keeping their eyes down, focusing on their duties.

Reynold went through the kitchen and into the library to wait for her. When Katarina rushed into the room, there was a puzzled expression on her face.

"Reynold," she said, "I thought you would not return for two more days." But she immediately saw the distress and anxiety on his face. "My darling, what is it?"

"I have never seen anything like it!" he said, his eyes darting about wildly. "A woman, the wife of one of my tenants, cast some kind of magical spell. Gunter is dead, Katarina. He was eaten up by rats!"

"Oh, my love," Katarina said, rushing to him. She threw her arms around him, and Reynold, in a feeling of desperation, held her tightly.

"I have never seen anything so horrifying!" he said.

"Do you want to go upstairs?" Katarina asked. He pushed her away and looked at her face.

"No, Katarina, I don't want to go upstairs. I just need a few moments to think." He paced for a few seconds, then looked at her again. "Will the Duke be here today?"

"No, Reynold, he is away on business in Wettin." She made a scoffing sound. "He brings me here to our country house, then he leaves to attend to business back at home."

"Good. I just need a quiet place to think." He paced a few more steps, then stopped, shaking his head. "I should have gone to my home."

"No," Katarina objected, "it's good that you came here. I'm glad you thought of me."

Reynold, still distracted, shook his head again. "Your whole kitchen staff saw me."

"That's alright. They know not to say anything."

"It's dangerous! I should go." Katarina started to object again, but she saw the determination on his face, and realized that he wasn't listening to her. "I'll try to come back in a couple of days."

Katarina stood there deflated as he rushed out of the library without another look at her.

Chapter 16

Max had assured Hayley that he didn't mind if she read more of the story at the table. Indeed, he seemed to enjoy watching her reaction to what she read. But while she was anxious to continue the story, she decided she didn't want to use their time together in this way.

"I'm not going to read anymore now," she said, placing the page she had just read face-down on the others. "We should be using this time to get to know each other."

"I agree," Max nodded. "I have told you about me. So it is your turn."

"You haven't told me *much* about you," Hayley muttered, "but okay. I was born in Denver, Colorado, where I live now. My mother is still there, and we're pretty close. I don't have any brothers or sisters. And, as I told you, I'm a music teacher.

"Speaking of family issues, my father put together investment opportunities, but it turned out he was cheating his investors and stealing their money. When the situation started catching up with him, he left and moved back to his native Germany. I was six years old, then, so I only know what I've been told about him.

"He came here to Hannover where he, apparently, continued his illegal activities. Eventually, it caught up with him again, one thing led to another, and he ended up shooting himself in the head, on two separate occasions, hoping to kill himself. But he failed both times."

Max had an odd look on his face, as if he thought something was funny, but didn't want to say anything.

"What is it?" Hayley asked.

"I am sorry. I know it is not funny that your father was suicidal. But it *is* almost comical how bad he was at it."

"Yeah," Hayley smiled, "he was kind of a loser, despite the wealth he accumulated. As it turned out, though, he lost a lot of it when the creditors and lawyers came after him."

"And he bequeathed the fruits of his criminal empire to you when he finally died?"

"No," Hayley scoffed. "It doesn't seem that he gave much thought to my existence at all. He left everything that remained after the lawyers got through with him to his nurse, Elsbeth, the one who cared for your mother." Max nodded. "But she thought that I should have it."

"That was very generous of her."

"Yes, it sure was."

"Did she know about the book?"

"No, she said she never went down into the basement."

"Oh, you found the book in the basement?" Max asked, a surprised look on his face.

"Well, it's a little more high-tech than it sounds. It was in a secret little sealed room off the wine cellar. I didn't know it at the time, but after being in the archive room at the university, I realize it was probably made specifically for safely storing things like that."

"Ah," Max nodded. "And you do not know where your father acquired the book?"

"No, I'm afraid not. I'm just hoping it wasn't one of his dishonest or illegal acquisitions, and I'd have to give it up."

The frown on Max's face implied his agreement.

§

"That's my car over there," Hayley said as they pulled into the parking lot at the university. Max glanced at her with an eyebrow raised.

"You have money, Hayley Hoffmann?"

"No," she scoffed, "I have stuff."

"Ah, of course, from your father." He pulled up next to the red vintage BMW and stopped. He looked at Hayley in the deepening twilight. "You are sure you do not want to see the *Georgengarten*?"

"Not tonight," Hayley replied. "The jet lag is still messing with me. But it sounds beautiful. I'd love to see it another time."

"Very well," he nodded. He leaned toward Hayley almost imperceptibly, looking at her tentatively, she thought, even shyly. She found it endearing, and she leaned the rest of the way until their lips met.

His kiss was soft and gentle, like his voice. When she pulled away, Hayley looked in his eyes and smiled. She got out of his car and settled down into hers. She looked at Max and he was still watching her. She smiled at him again as she started up her car and drove away.

Chapter 17

Abelard, the baker was exhausted. He had never seen so many rats. He had spent most of the day trying to kill them or shoo them out the door. It had proven almost hopeless.

When they had first shown up, he had been fortunate enough to locate where most of them were coming from, a small hole in the wall beside his oven. He got some rags and stuffed the hole tightly, no doubt a temporary solution, but at least it gave him time to concentrate on the rats already in his shop.

He used a broom to start with, pushing the rats toward the back door and into the alleyway, but they were quick, many of them scrambling out from in front of the broom. With those he was able to push to the door, as soon as he opened it and pushed the rats out, others rushed in. After that, he kept the door closed. He started swinging the broom harder and faster, and succeeded in at least stunning some of the rats by slinging them against the wall. Using a sheet pan to scoop them up, he tossed them out the back window.

He realized, though, that he wasn't solving the problem. Stunned rats could regain consciousness and continue wreaking havoc. So, he began hitting the rats with a shovel. He killed several this way, but was horrified to witness other rats suddenly swarm over his victims, stripping their skeletons clean in a matter of seconds.

Finally, though, after several hours of work, he seemed to get rid of them. Through the front window of his shop, he saw people running, or walking erratically, and he knew the rats were still around. But, at least he could rest for a few minutes.

He looked up when he heard the bell on the door ring, and Lars Delbruch entered his shop. Along with several rats scurrying around his feet.

"Yes, Lars," Abelard said wearily, "what can I do for you?"

"It's about the loaf of bread you sold me this morning," Lars replied. "I know it's not your fault," he added, glancing around at the rats that had come in with him. He unwrapped the paper from the loaf, showing Abelard the loaf that had the end cut off of it. Embedded in the bread, cut in half by Lars' bread knife, was the baked carcass of a rat. "But I don't think I should be charged for this."

"No, of course not," Abelard said, repelled by the sight. "I am so sorry." Lars shook his head.

"I don't blame you, Abelard. It's these accursed vermin!"

Abelard pressed a groschen into Lars' hand. Lars looked at it, then looked up at Abelard.

"This is not what I paid you."

"It is what you paid me," Abelard replied, "and extra for your trouble to bring back the loaf. And I would give you another loaf, but I've not had a chance to do any more baking."

"Thank you, Abelard. You're a good man." Lars turned toward the door, then stopped and turned back. "There is perhaps, one good result from all of this. Did you hear about what happened to Gunter, von Hoffmann's lackey?" Abelard shook his head. "He was evicting a couple this morning. Rats swarmed over him and ate him up. They picked his bones clean in just a couple of minutes."

"It's too bad they didn't do the same to von Hoffmann," replied the baker with a grieved smile.

"Yes, many of us have thought the same thing."

"If that truly happened," Abelard pondered, "I wonder why the rats have not tried to eat you or me."

"What I heard from someone who saw it happen," Lars replied, "was that the wife invoked the rats as they were being evicted. It was Adelaide Schüller, the daughter of Rosamund the witch. It looked as if she was trying to direct them toward von Hoffmann, but was killed before she could complete the spell." Lars shrugged his shoulders. "Perhaps they were brought here to make that initial kill, and having done so, are now roaming free without command or purpose. And Adelaide is dead, now, and unable to call them back."

"How fortunate for us," Abelard said sardonically.

"Yes," Lars agreed. He held up the groschen in his hand. "Thank you, Abelard." He went out the front door, as a few more rats scurried in.

§

The river Weser snaked lazily toward the northwest through Hamelin. Certain locations on its banks were sought out by some of the women of the town for doing their laundry chores, and for exchanging the latest gossip. It was now also a welcome getaway from the rats overrunning the town.

Greta, the young laundress employed by the Duchess Katarina, had wash tubs and hot water aplenty available to her, but she was about to burst with her news. Besides, the rats were plaguing their estate now, as well. She decided that a trip to the river was called for.

"You actually saw this?" her friend Ella asked as she stopped scrubbing her husband's shirt for a moment, a shocked expression on her face.

"With my own two eyes!" Greta replied. "Baron von Hoffmann was holding Her Grace in his arms in a most familiar way! And I'm told that he has spent some very late hours at the house. In fact, I understand that some suspect he has even stayed through the night and slipped out in the early morning."

"And the Duke knows nothing of this?" Of course, Ella knew the answer, since von Hoffmann was still alive.

"No, not a bit of it," Greta insisted. "Mind you, you can't tell anyone about this. I'm only telling you because you're such a good friend."

"Of course," Ella said, looking a little offended at the thought that she would betray her confidence. She wrung out the shirt and placed it in the basket with the rest of her laundry. "Well, good day, Greta. It was good to see you."

"And you, Ella," Greta smiled. Ella stood up and stretched her back. Then, she picked up the basket and walked away. Greta squeezed the water out of the linen towel she was cleaning and placed it in her basket. A few moments later, the spot next to her was filled by Heidi, a young recent bride. Greta had seen her a few times, but didn't really know her.

"You're Heidi, aren't you?" she asked.

"Yes, I am," Heidi replied, her pink cheeks bulging with her smile. "And you are?"

"Greta. I work for Her Grace, Duchess Katarina."

"Oh, how nice!" Heidi began unloading the large basket of clothing she had brought with her.

"You won't believe what I saw this morning!" Greta said, a conspiratorial tone in her voice.

§

The project was going slowly. Cort had stacked several lengths of oak from his drying shed into his work area, but they were still rough and needed to be planed. Elysande, despite her obvious discomfort, had required little of his attention, and Bergh, while unable to assist him, stayed out of his way.

Still, when the rats started showing up, it was distracting, to say the least. Elysande, to her credit, did not scream or try to hide, like many other women might do, but she did draw her feet up when a couple of the beasts became a little too sociable. They had never seen rats so comfortable in the presence of people.

Swatting a rat out of the way, Cort sat down on the stack of lumber in his work area and wiped the sweat from his face. He looked at Elysande for a moment, who looked curiously back at him.

"I don't think you should stay here," he said. "People will talk."

Elysande smiled at the thought, though the smile didn't show through the swelling. People had been "talking" about her for nearly her whole life. While she had struggled to leave that life behind, she wasn't afraid of being the subject of gossip. At the same time, she didn't want to bring disrepute upon a good and respectable man.

That thought in itself surprised her. She didn't make it a practice to trust men. She knew what they were usually after. In fact, she had counted on it back when she was still in business.

But Cort had brought her inside his home and cleaned her up without taking advantage of her. He had proven himself, so far, to be a kind and decent man. She was still cautious, guarded, but she didn't want to soil his reputation.

"You're right," she nodded, and Bergh conveyed her words to Cort. "But I don't know where to go."

"I can take you back to the convent," Cort suggested, but she shook her head.

"No, I've discovered that the life of a nun is not for me. I just don't know where I can go, or what else I can do." Or rather she knew what she could do, but she didn't want to go back to that. She pulled the corner of the blanket up off the ground, shaking a rat off of it.

"I know what you can do," Bergh piped up. "There's plenty of room at my house. My father's hardly ever there. And I know he still has some of my mother's clothes packed away. You could see if any of it fits you."

"I don't know," Elysande replied hesitantly. She knew who Reynold von Hoffmann was, by reputation. In contrast to her thoughts about Cort, she wasn't worried about besmirching von Hoffmann's character. Indeed, she knew that he had been a customer of hers a few years ago, and as she recalled, he was not a nice man, even beyond his business demeanor.

"No, that may not be the best choice," Cort agreed diplomatically. He thought for a few moments. "I have an idea. I can make a little more room in my shed. I use it for storing my tools and drying lumber, but I've removed much of the lumber for this job. I can move some of the tools out of there, too, set up a cot for you. It's just turned June, so with a blanket or two, it should be warm enough."

"Thank you, Herr Rottweill," she replied.

"Please, call me Cort."

"Of course. And you may call me Ely."

"You may not want to thank me just yet, Ely," Cort continued, cocking an eyebrow at her. Ely looked suspiciously at him. "You should stay out of sight as long as you're here, at least until you decide what you want to do. It would not do for the townspeople to see you here, even in my shed."

He looked down at her body, still wrapped in the blanket, and he remembered.

"We must get you some clothes, too." He looked at Bergh. "Perhaps we could use some of your mother's clothing."

Chapter 18

Hayley placed the page face-down on the growing stack of papers on her nightstand. She was about to turn the light off when her phone pinged with a text message. The phone number was familiar, but there was no name displayed. However, she knew when she saw the message.

"Still want to see Hannover? I still want to show you."

"Hi, Peter. Feeling a little better each day. Maybe tomorrow." She felt like such a wimp. It wasn't even nine o'clock yet, and still light outside. But she had lasted a little longer than the day before.

"Great! I'll be available after 1 pm."

"I'll call you. Good night, Peter."

§

Hayley met Peter in the parking lot of the university, where he begged her to let him drive her car again. Since she didn't know her way around town, she was happy to oblige.

About eight minutes later, though, he seemed chagrined as he pulled into a parking structure.

"When am I going to learn? I should have taken you to Hamburg or Leipzig. Then I could open her up and see how she really drives."

"Maybe another time," Hayley smiled.

"You know," Peter said, "a few years ago, one of these babies sold for 2.4 million."

"Shit! The insurance is going to kill me!"

Peter snickered at her reaction.

"Face it, Hayley, you're kind of in that 1% they talk about back home."

Hayley sighed and rolled her eyes.

"So, where did you bring me?" she asked.

"Well, it's lunch time. This is where a lot of the locals come for groceries and other items."

"You brought me to a grocery store?"

"Calling the *Markthalle* a grocery store," Peter grinned, "is like calling a 1958 convertible BMW 507 a car."

They walked into the vibrant place, and Hayley was overwhelmed with the sights, sounds and smells. There were expansive displays of produce of every color imaginable, long display cases of meats and seafood, glass cases of cheeses, a mind-boggling assortment of breads and other bakery items, wines, and numerous things she couldn't begin to recognize. And mixed in among all of it were a number of restaurants and cafes.

"Oh my god," Hayley raved as she tried to take it all in, "it's like they started with a food court and decided they didn't even need the mall after all."

They spent time walking up and down aisles, looking at what was available.

"I suppose this is all really expensive," Hayley said.

"Actually, it's cheaper than most regular grocery stores. That's why so many locals come here."

It was educational for Hayley, as she recognized some of the food items she had seen in her pantry and refrigerator. With someone to talk to about it, she was able to get a better idea of what she should do with it. And she purchased a couple of kitchen items that she decided she couldn't do without.

After nearly an hour, though, Hayley's stomach was protesting. They stopped at a sandwich café for lunch and sat down at a table facing out into the market so they could continue people watching.

After they finished eating, Peter leaned toward Hayley.

"So, do you want to look around some more?"

"You know," Hayley replied, "I think my senses are a little overloaded now. Maybe we can go someplace not quite so enclosed. Someplace quiet." Then, her expression perked up a little. "Someplace old. I love old things."

"Of course you do," Peter said, his dark eyes twinkling. "I think I know just the place." He guided her into the aisle and through the crowd, toward the door to the parking structure, with his hand on the small of her back. He opened the car door for her, then got in on the driver's side.

"Dammit," Peter said.

"What?"

"Where we're going is only about a minute or two away from here."

Hayley smiled at his frustration.

"I can't help it that Hannover is so convenient."

Peter grinned at her as he started up the car and pulled out of the parking garage. He drove just a little ways down *Leinstraße* and Hayley pointed at a street sign bearing the street name.

"How do you say that?" she asked.

"Line-strass-uh," Peter replied. Hayley repeated it, like she did when listening to her language course. "It literally means Flax Street," Peter said. "No idea what flax has to do with the street."

He continued a short distance until the road narrowed even more than it already was. They bumped over cobblestones for a short distance, then back onto asphalt.

"We're in luck," he said as he pulled into an empty parking space on the street. They got out of the car and Peter joined Hayley on the sidewalk as she gazed in awe at the old buildings lining the right side of the street.

"It's like we're in a storybook," she said quietly.

The right side of the street was lined with old half-timbered buildings, dark wood timbers exposed against the white surface, some with stunning and quaint architectural details.

"Hannover used to have a large Old Town area," Peter said as they walked northwest along *Burgstraße*. "During World War II, America and England did something like eighty-eight bombing raids on Hannover. As you might imagine, all that carpet-bombing destroyed a lot of the buildings. Some time back, the city decided to embark on a pretty ambitious endeavor. They took the remaining facades in Old Town and moved them all together here along this street, and into this little square." He motioned into *Ballhofplatz* as they came alongside it. "So I guess you could call this the new Old Town."

"Oh," Hayley breathed, grabbing Peter's arm as if she needed help standing up. "I love it!" she whispered.

The square was lined with the half-timbered buildings, some covered with ivy, and truly looked like an illustration from an old book of Mother Goose nursery rhymes she had as a child.

They wandered at a leisurely pace around the square, looking in shops, and taking frequent breaks for Hayley to admire and rhapsodize about the architecture. By the time they came back around toward the street, Peter noticed Hayley looking around almost regretfully.

"We don't have to go just yet," he said.

She looked up at him and smiled. The tea shop in front of them, in an ivy-covered building, was inviting, as was the seating area in front of it under the awning.

"Suddenly," she said, "I'd love a cup of tea."

Her grateful smile was so captivating, he couldn't help smiling back at her. They went inside, both reveling in the fresh-brewed smells. Peter ordered a double espresso, while Hayley got a Tiger Spice Chai.

They relaxed under the awning with their beverages, sitting facing the square so that Hayley could continue to enjoy the sights. There was a chill in the air, and clouds were gathering overhead. After a few minutes, it started to rain, just a light sprinkle, but it was enough for others in the area to seek shelter. Many decided it was a good time for tea, and Hayley was happy for the tea shop.

"I think this is one of the most beautiful places I've ever seen," Hayley said.

"Wow," Peter said, "I was thinking about taking you to the *Georgengarten*, but I'm glad I decided on this."

"Oh, yes," Hayley said, "I am, too. Max wanted to take me to the *Georgengarten*."

"Really." Peter replied. It sounded more like a belligerent statement than a question, and his voice sounded a little deflated. Hayley happened to be looking at his face when he said it, and noticed his expression.

"What is it?" she asked, a note of frustration in her voice. "I've seen that same expression cross Max's face when I've mentioned you."

"You've seen it, too?" Peter replied, turning toward her anxiously. "I was afraid I was just imagining it!"

"So, there really is something going on between you two."

Peter sighed and looked back toward the quaint buildings and sidewalk cafes of *Ballhofplatz*.

"I don't want to spoil this for you," he said.

"Peter, I like you." Then, in a cautious tone, she added, "And, I like Max. The fact that there's something like this between you two kind of spoils it for me."

Peter looked down at his espresso for a few moments, still steaming in the cool air, then drew his eyes back up to Hayley and sighed again.

"I hate to say anything, because I'm afraid it'll sound like I'm boasting." He paused for a few moments to gather his thoughts. "A few months ago, I turned in a paper about the emigration of Germans to the New World in the seventeenth century. You know, they helped the English found Jamestown, Virginia, and also New Amsterdam, which would later become New York City.

"A few weeks later, Professor Schiller published an article about seventeenth-century German immigrants in America, much of which was copied word-for-word from my paper."

"Oh, Peter!" Hayley sympathized.

"Yeah. I know most students don't even realize that their professors do anything other than teach their classes." Peter looked down at his cup again. "But I guess I'm a nerd, at least where German history is concerned. I read everything I can find about it. So, I admit I was a little pissed when I found that."

"Well, of course you were!"

"I don't know whether to say anything or not. I don't want to risk my grades. I mean, he gave me good marks for that paper before he lifted it as his own."

"I'm so sorry, Peter."

"Please don't say anything to him about this," Peter implored, looking back up at Hayley, "at least until I figure out what to do about it."

"Of course not," Hayley said. "You have my word."

"Thanks." Peter sighed again and drained the last of his espresso.

"Well," Hayley said, "I guess we can go anytime."

Peter took her to an Italian restaurant for dinner. Hayley was sorry to see that his mood seemed to be sagging a little for the rest of the evening. While she was glad to know what was going on between him and Max, she regretted bringing it up, for Peter's sake.

It was nearly ten o'clock when she got back home. Peter's disquiet was still on her mind, so she looked forward to the distraction of crawling into bed and reading the next chapter of the book.

Chapter 19

Elysande succeeded in settling in quickly at Cort's place. The rats were as much of a problem there as they were elsewhere, but the fact that both Ely and Cort were relatively unconcerned helped. When they got into Cort's food, he took steps to protect it from them, but for the most part, they just tried to ignore the vermin.

Cort took time away from his job for von Hoffmann to create some barriers to keep the rats out of their beds. They consisted primarily of boards attached horizontally along the top of the bedsteads as a ledge, to prevent the rats from being able to climb up and over. He figured that only the most determined rat would be able to grip its claws into the bottom of the horizontal surface and get into the beds. Since the beds contained no food to attract them, there had, as yet, been no rat that accepted the challenge.

Bergh had succeeded in getting a couple of his mother's dresses for Ely, though her favorite clothing turned out to be a tunic and a pair of breeches that Cort had purchased for her. He had said that he was buying them as a gift for Bergh to allay the curiosity of the shopkeeper.

Her hair was already cut short, something she had chosen to do when she joined the Magdelens. From a distance, at least, she could pass as a boy helping Cort with his work. Since few people visited Cort, Ely went largely unnoticed.

Except by Cort.

§

"What did they say?" Ely asked anxiously when Cort returned. A few days had passed, and the swelling had gone down enough that he was able to read her lips, though her eye and the left side of her face were still badly discolored.

At Ely's urging, Cort had saddled up his horse and ridden to the convent, to inform them that she was alright but had chosen to remain outside the order. They didn't seem surprised.

"They thanked me for letting them know," Cort replied as he unbuckled the saddle. The horse snorted nervously as a rat skittered past his hooves.

"Who did you speak to?"

"A Mother Tabitha."

He slid the blanket off his horse's back and draped it over the rail of the stall in the stable. The horse shifted back and forth as another rat scampered toward the other one.

"Ah," Ely replied. She looked downward, clearly hoping for more, but not wanting to continue bothering Cort. But Cort didn't seem at all bothered by it. He smiled at her and enlarged on his remarks.

"She wished you well and hoped that you find happiness, preferably within the bounds of scriptural guidelines." Ely smiled and wiped away a tear.

Suddenly, the horse reared up slightly, stomping back down. Surprised, Cort looked down and saw the tail of a rat sticking out from under his hoof.

"I had hoped that I could stay with them," Ely continued, "and start a new life of chastity and piety," she mused.

"Your chastity and piety can continue here," Cort replied a little defensively.

"Yes!" Ely replied quickly, nodding her head. "Yes, but I don't wish to be a burden on anybody while embarking on my new life."

"You are no burden," Cort said softly.

Despite wearing the clothing of a man, she was, quite clearly, a beautiful woman. On the rare occasions when someone came around, she kept her distance, and Cort thought that was wise. Nobody with eyes in their head could possibly mistake this creature for a boy.

In fact, in the last couple of days, Cort had begun to worry about his own chastity and piety.

§

Late in June, a traveler arrived in Hamelin, dusty and weary from the road. The man was tall and gaunt, and dressed in clothing of many colors, as if pieced together from several other unrelated garments. He spoke to few people as he made his way through town to the inn, but he seemed to notice everything.

By this time, the rats had overrun the town for nearly three weeks. The townspeople had succeeded in killing many of them, more than they could deal with, and the smell rising from the piles of carcasses was nearly overwhelming. Still, the rats reproduced at an alarming rate. For every rat that was killed, it seemed to be replaced by at least two more.

Many of the townspeople wore bandages around ankles and hands, some showing red and festering wounds from rat bites. The general mood was dark, gloomy, angry.

That evening, the visitor stood in the town square and reached into the pack he had carried on his back. He pulled out a long, narrow bag made of colorful silk. He loosened the drawstring, and from the bag, he drew out a shining silver pipe of beautiful workmanship.

Few people paid attention to him as he placed the flute up to his mouth, but then, he began playing a sweet and pleasing tune. The music soothed the daunted and disheartened townsfolk, and without exception, they all stopped to listen. Despite the bites and the dark moods, for a few moments, they paid attention to nothing but the sweet sounds coming out of the flute.

If anybody present had been able to look at anyone other than the gifted piper, they would have seen tears in the eyes of many of the listeners.

The music drew others from their homes and shops, and soon, most of the town was gathered before the piper. They even seemed oblivious to the rodents gamboling about at their feet. When the piper finished the sweet tune, there was an audible sigh from all the people crowding the square.

They all stayed there, looking expectantly at him, hoping for another tune. Instead, the piper spoke.

"Gentle people of Hamelin," he said, "I could not help but notice the horrid infestation you are being forced to endure." His voice was soft with feeling and empathy, yet it seemed to carry to every ear in the square. "I am happy to tell you that I can remove these vermin so that they will not bother you again."

Mayor Hildebrandt stepped forward out of the crowd, approaching the piper.

"Are you speaking truth, piper?" he asked.

"Indeed," the piper smiled.

Every head in the square turned anxiously toward the Mayor.

"By what method can you possibly rid our town of so great an infestation?"

"The method is my own, one which I developed. For the price of a thousand guilders, your town will be free of rats."

Mayor Hildebrandt looked around at the townspeople surrounding him. Several heads were nodding, silently pleading with him to accept the piper's offer.

"How can we be sure you can accomplish this?" he asked.

"If I do not accomplish it," the piper shrugged, "I do not get paid."

Mayor Hildebrandt sighed looking at the beseeching expressions of the people.

"We are a humble town. I'm afraid we don't have a thousand guilders available in the town's coffers for something like this."

"The solution is a simple one, Your Honor," the piper replied. "Assuming your residents are willing, collect from the population an amount, based on each one's financial worth and ability to pay, that would total the necessary price."

Again, Mayor Hildebrandt looked at the people around him, and again, several heads were nodding.

"Alright," the Mayor replied, "we will pay your price." The sound of a collective sigh rose from the crowd. "When will you do this?"

"You have a large job ahead of you, Your Honor," the piper replied, "as do I. You spend tomorrow collecting the money from your people, and I shall spend it preparing for the task. On the following morning, I will rid your town of its infestation. When the job is done, and only then, shall you pay me."

Mayor Hildebrandt stepped forward, holding his right hand out toward the piper. The piper smiled and readily shook the Mayor's hand.

Chapter 20

Ely proved to be a good helper when Cort needed a second pair of hands. She also had a good eye for detail, and gave helpful suggestions, many of which he applied in the construction of von Hoffmann's table and chairs.

By now, the construction of the table was complete, and it was standing in the workshop of his cottage, protected from the weather. He was starting on the chairs now, and since it was a pleasant day, he was working out in his courtyard. He was planning to create the framework and the seats for all of the chairs, then carve intricate backs that would match details on the table.

As was often the case, Ely was sitting on one of the stools that Cort kept in his courtyard, watching him work. They didn't talk much since he had to be watching her to understand what she said. Still, whenever he took a break, they would talk, and they had drawn close over the last few weeks.

Cort, his blond hair pulled back out of his way, sat on the other stool as he shaped and smoothed a mortise socket he had carved in the stile of the chair. He picked up the side rail which already had the tenon carved into the end, and he tested the fit. The tenon fit easily but snugly into the mortise, and he looked up at Ely and smiled. She was looking down at the ground and frowning.

He looked around. There were a couple of rats in the courtyard, but they were leaving Cort and Ely alone. He looked back up at her.

"What's wrong, Ely?"

She quickly looked up at him as if waking from a dream. She smiled at him, but it wasn't a very convincing one. She shook her head and started to say it was nothing, but she knew he wouldn't believe her.

"It's just that you've been so good to me," she finally said.

"No wonder you're upset," Cort said, a look of feigned anguish on his face. "I'm sorry." Ely managed a real smile, then continued.

"I don't feel like I've been completely honest with you." She paused and Cort put the chair parts down to focus his attention on her.

"Ely," he said, "you don't have to tell me anything you don't want to."

"I do want to, though," she said. "I want to be completely open and honest with you. At the same time, I don't want you to hate me."

Cort scoffed and shook his head.

"I don't think I could ever hate you," he said softly.

She gave him a sad disbelieving look, then she took a deep breath.

"I was a prostitute," she finally blurted out, her eyes closed tightly as if she was afraid to see Cort's reaction. "I used to stand near the southern gate and . . ."

She paused again, unable to continue, as a tear squeezed between her eyelids. Cort's response surprised her.

"I know," he said.

Ely quickly looked up at him and wiped the tear away.

"You know?" she asked incredulously.

"I know what a Magdalen is," he said simply.

"But," Ely cast about for a response. "Then, why have you been so good to me?"

"Because you're a good person," he replied simply. Ely scoffed.

"I was a prostitute," she repeated, as if that easily refuted his argument.

"You were a nun," he corrected.

"A failed nun," she said.

Cort shook his head as he looked intently into her eyes.

"Everyone makes mistakes," he said.

"I committed fornication for money," she stressed.

"And you were sorry enough to give it up and try to become a nun." Ely sighed as if she wasn't able to accept his absolution. "I killed a little boy," he finally said harshly. "I'm sorry," he immediately said, "my anger is for me, not for you." Ely still looked as if he had struck her.

"You killed a little boy?" she repeated quietly.

Cort took a deep breath and related the story of his final battle, the one that visited him in his dreams so many nights.

"Oh, Cort," she breathed when he had finished.

"There is not a single day that passes without me seeing his shocked face as he lay there bleeding into the snow and the mud, the recognition slowly fading from his eyes."

"Still," Ely said, hoping to assuage the grief he still felt, "it was an accident. You did not choose to kill him. I chose my occupation."

"Whether you chose it, or you felt you had no other choice, it was also your choice to stop and join the convent."

"But I left them, too."

"You went from one extreme to the other," Cort said. "It was a noble endeavor, but it was too great a change to accomplish all at once." A rat started trying to climb his leg and, angry at the interruption, Cort swatted it against the wall of the courtyard, killing it. "And a few days ago," he continued, "you said you wanted to continue your new life of chastity and piety." He raised his eyebrows and nodded as if he knew he had won the argument.

Ely looked at him, wiping fresh tears from her eyes, and she shook her head.

"Though I know I don't deserve it, I hope you can always see me in such a light."

She had never felt anything like the attachment she was beginning to feel for Cort. Every man she had ever been with had been a simple business deal, a brief contact with a payment at the end. This feeling was so foreign to her.

She wanted to go to him and hold him, be held by him. She wanted to kiss him, but she feared that if she did, her hoped-for life of chastity and piety would simply vanish in a brief moment of ecstasy.

Her decision was made when she heard footsteps approaching the cottage. She quickly jumped up and slipped through the door, closing it quietly behind her.

Cort sat there for a few moments, looking at the door in blank bewilderment, until he saw two men at the entrance of his walled courtyard. One carried a small leather bag, the other a small book.

"Cort Rottweill?" asked the man with the bag. Both of his ankles and a thumb were bandaged.

"Yes," he replied, standing up and approaching them.

"We are here at the Mayor's request. Have you heard about the man who claims he can rid our town of rats?"

"No, I have not."

"He will do the job tomorrow morning for a thousand guilders," the man replied. "We're collecting from all the residents of Hamelin based on their ability to pay. Can you contribute four groschen?"

"Yes, I certainly can!" Cort replied enthusiastically. "Excuse me." He went into the cottage to a jar where he kept a little cash. He passed Ely on his way back to the door, and on a whim, he kissed her on the cheek. Before she could react, he went back outside.

The man with the bag had just kicked a rat away from his foot. It was stunned and Cort kicked it hard against the wall, killing it instantly, where it landed not far from the one he had killed earlier. He smiled and paid the men.

"Thank you, sir," the man said. He dropped the coins into the bag while the other man made a note in the little book. "God willing, we will have a clean town again soon!"

Cort watched them walk away. He was still smiling, and he realized it wasn't because of the prospect of being rid of the rats.

He remembered the softness of Ely's cheek against his lips.

Chapter 21

Despite the fact that she loved her job, during the school year, Hayley was always ready for Friday. Elementary school kids were a delight, but they were exhausting, so the end of the week was always welcome. The weekend gave her time to recharge, so that she was ready to get back to the kids by Monday morning.

During the summer, without the usual weekly structure, she would sometimes lose track of what day it was. Since she had been in Germany, in unfamiliar surroundings, that effect was especially in play.

But she had no plans, no place she had to be, so when she woke up, she lounged in bed for a while, corresponding with friends through email, text messages and Facebook. She felt a little unmotivated, and Peter's mood from the evening before was weighing on her.

She was upset at Max for what he did to Peter, and while she wanted to take him to task for it, she knew she wouldn't. First of all, she had promised Peter that she wouldn't say anything. But there was also the fact that Max was translating her book for her. One selfish little corner of her brain didn't want to possibly upset him and make him stop working on it.

Still, another dark thought occurred to her. Peter had suggested that the book was worth millions of dollars. If Max had seen no problem with plagiarizing Peter's work for recognition or tenure, how willing might he be to steal a historical artifact that could make him rich beyond his dreams?

Hayley shook her head and got out of bed. She didn't like thinking bad thoughts about others. Hayley always tried to think the best of people, to give them the benefit of the doubt.

She was startled when her phone rang, and pleasantly surprised when she recognized Peter's number.

"Hello, Peter," she smiled.

"Hey," he said in his easy, relaxed manner, "I just wanted to apologize about last night. I know I spoiled our evening, and I'm sorry."

"You didn't spoil anything," Hayley protested, "and you don't need to apologize. You had a valid complaint, and it's completely natural to feel the way you do about it."

"That's very understanding of you." Peter sounded relieved.

"You know," Hayley said, "it's quite a coincidence that you just called about this. I was just thinking about last night, and about you and Max."

"Oh?" Peter's tone was uncertain.

"I know you know him better than I do, but I've spent about the same amount of time with him as I have with you. I'm usually a pretty good judge of character, and he really seems like a very decent person." Her voice took on a more cautious tone.

"Maybe he didn't remember your assignment, and he wrote what he thought were original ideas or conclusions. I mean, he'd probably be horrified if he realized that he had published your work as his own."

"Hmm," Peter replied. Hayley couldn't tell if he was open to the idea or doubtful. "I suppose it's possible," he finally conceded. "I found other articles that he had published that seemed to borrow heavily from other papers I had turned in. But I suppose I can accept the possibility that I'm an influential but otherwise forgettable writer."

"Smartass," Hayley smiled. "You know that's not what I'm saying."

"I know. You're saying I should give him the benefit of the doubt and talk to him about it."

"No, I'm not even saying that. I mean the benefit of the doubt is a good idea, but whether he's told about it or not is entirely up to you. If you decide he should be told, it should come from you. I promised I won't say anything to him, and I intend to keep that promise."

"Thank you."

"Of course." Hayley grinned. "So, you called me to apologize and I hijacked the conversation. I'm sorry."

"Well, I didn't call *only* to apologize. After last night, I feel like I owe you a better night out, one where I'm not acting like a moody little child."

"You weren't that bad," Hayley insisted, "but that would be nice."

"Are you free this evening?"

"After checking my busy schedule, I see that I do have a bit of time where I can pencil you in this evening."

"Now, who's the smartass?" Peter replied, and Hayley could hear the smile in his voice. "I'll pick you up at 6:00."

"I'm looking forward to it."

She smiled as she disconnected, and she realized that she really was.

Chapter 22

Shafts of dim, premature light shoved their way upwards through the clouds from the sun's position below the eastern horizon. The sky was beginning to brighten, but it was still dark on the ground as a lone figure quietly took his place at the edge of town.

As if concentrating his power and attention, he took several deep breaths and loosened his arms and neck. Finally, he lifted the silver pipe in his hands up to his lips. He took a breath and began playing a jaunty tune as he walked along the road into town.

The sweet notes drifted out on the early morning breeze, finding their way into all the houses, and into the sensitive ears of the vermin dwelling in them. As the piper walked through Hamelin, his steps unconsciously matching the tempo of the tune, there was a light rustling sound in some of the nearer houses.

Emerging from the deep shadows of the town, smaller shadows coalesced into the forms of rats tumbling out of the houses, climbing over each other, and over the piles of their dead brethren, to get to the piper. As he marched along the cobblestones of the street, the rats followed for no reason their little minds could understand.

The sky was lightening as the piper continued through town, and the rustling sound grew in volume as more rats were drawn out of the shops and alleys. The piper turned onto different streets, apparently at random, each time adding more rats to the roiling mass following along behind him.

In some houses, he could see candlelight, as people were rising for their day, or perhaps awoken by the sound of the rats scurrying from their houses. Faces pressed against their windows, watching in disbelief as the streets were completely covered with the dark, churning waves of rodents following closely on the piper's heels.

By the time the piper reached the other end of town, if anybody had wanted to come outside, they couldn't have without crushing multiple rats with each step, so great was his following. The street was carpeted with rodents jostling for a position closer to the piper and the bewitching and captivating tune he played. He continued his march off the road and down toward the Weser.

At the river's edge, he stepped aside, and he added a little trill to the tune he played. At that, the rats began running past him, racing toward the river, tumbling over each other to reach it. In moments, the slow-moving river was boiling with innumerable rats churning, drowning, finally washed away toward the north.

§

Like the rats before them, everyone swarmed out of their houses to greet the piper as he came back into town. His gaunt face stretched into a smile as he accepted their thanks and adulation. The people parted to allow him to pass, but then, without his needing to play his pipe, they followed him.

He stopped at the town square where Mayor Hildebrandt met him, holding a bag of money in his hands. The piper smiled again as he shook the Mayor's outstretched hand.

"Sir," the Mayor said, "we, the people of Hamelin, wish to express our deepest gratitude to you. We humbly and gladly give you our hand in friendship, and this payment for your kind services."

The piper nodded, seeming a little uncomfortable with the continued attention, but he accepted the bag that the Mayor handed him. He loosened the drawstring and glanced inside, but then, his smile vanished. He pulled the bag open wider, tilting it to allow the early morning sunlight to shine inside.

"Your Honor," he said, his voice thin and tight, "this bag is full of groschen. This cannot total anywhere near a thousand guilders."

"You must be mistaken, sir," the Mayor said. "I only received it recently, but I was assured that it is the full amount you asked for."

"I assure you it is not," the piper replied icily, "and that I am not mistaken. I will not be cheated out of what I am due by a passel of simple-minded country folk."

Mayor Hildebrandt was taken aback by the piper's tone and accusation.

"Sir, we are neither simple-minded nor cheaters," the Mayor said indignantly. "We are honest people and are happy to pay our debts."

"Well, you have not done so in this case," the piper said, angrily pulling the drawstring closed. "But you will pay, most dearly."

As the piper turned and pushed his way through the crowd, Mayor Hildebrandt stood there looking after him, bewildered by the sudden change in the man's demeanor.

§

He was certain that they must have paid the piper the agreed-upon amount, but just in case a mistake had been made, Mayor Hildebrandt spent the day in his office, poring over the documents that his collectors had brought back. He laboriously noted each citizen, and added up the amounts that they had all donated toward the cause, consulting numerous town records to be certain he had accounted for everyone.

The shadows shifted position from his window as the sun passed overhead, and by the time the sun hovered near the western horizon, Mayor Hildebrandt had discovered the issue. One person was unaccounted for.

Since the contribution amounts were calculated by each individual's estimated financial standing and ability to pay, it would leave a vast deficit if the area's wealthiest citizen and landowner failed to pay his fair share. But as Mayor Hildebrandt scanned back through the documents, he found no record of Reynold von Hoffmann having paid anything at all.

No wonder the piper had been angry. He was correct. He had not been paid what they agreed on. The Mayor decided that he needed to speak to von Hoffmann right away.

§

"Very odd," Mayor Hildebrandt muttered to himself again. It had been a repeated refrain since he left von Hoffmann's estate. He had been greeted at the door by Renilda, von Hoffmann's housekeeper. When pressed, Renilda had finally revealed to him that von Hoffmann was at the Duke's country home.

The Mayor knew that the Duke was not at his country home, so why would von Hoffmann be there?

"Most unusual," he muttered again as he tied his horse to a post near the front door of the Duke's home.

"Mayor Hildebrandt," greeted Gerhard, the Duke's butler upon answering the Mayor's knock.

"I must speak with Baron von Hoffmann right away."

"Baron von Hoffmann, sir?" Gerhard's eyes glanced nervously about for a moment.

"That's right. I was told he was here."

"Yes, Your Honor," Gerhard capitulated with a respectful head tilt. "Please come in."

Mayor Hildebrandt entered the expansive front hall as Gerhard left him to climb one of the curved staircases that ascended each side of the entry. The Mayor had never been in such a grand house. The area was completely awash with exquisite tapestries and gilded surfaces.

A few minutes later, Reynold von Hoffmann appeared at the upper landing, nervously lagging behind Gerhard as he adjusted his clothing. For the briefest moment, Mayor Hildebrandt thought he saw the Duchess peek around the corner after them.

"Mayor Hildebrandt," von Hoffmann said as he reached the entry. "What a pleasant surprise." His tone of voice confirmed that it was indeed a surprise, but anything but a pleasant one. "What can I do for you?"

"I've come to collect your portion of the piper's payment for removing the rats from Hamelin. You seem to have forgotten to pay your share."

"Ah, Your Honor, you are mistaken. I did not forget. I did not pay it because I felt that it was not a fair charge. My home, outside of Hamelin as it is, was not so greatly affected by the rat infestation. Besides, I am seldom there, anyway."

"Yes," Mayor Hildebrandt said, "I see that." Catching the veiled accusation in the Mayor's voice, von Hoffmann stiffened a bit. "The town agreed on the amount that was to be paid to the piper to rid the town of rats. You are obligated to pay your fair share."

"I'm sorry, Your Honor, but I was not involved in this agreement. Nobody asked for my opinion on the matter."

"That may be," the mayor replied, "but regardless, it was a majority vote."

"I truly am sorry, Your Honor," von Hoffmann said with an increasingly irritated tone, "but you will have to satisfy this piper character without a donation from me."

Mayor Hildebrandt looked at von Hoffmann through narrowed eyelids, and he shook his head.

"Please excuse me for interrupting you," the Mayor finally said. "I will allow you to get back to your hostess." The emphasis he placed on the last word left no mistaking of his meaning.

Before von Hoffmann could reply, Mayor Hildebrandt turned and left.

Chapter 23

"Seriously?" Hayley thought, "a cliffhanger?" She took a deep breath and pulled herself up into a sitting position when her stomach grumbled loudly at her. She placed this last page she had onto the stack on her nightstand. She wondered how close Max was to completing his translation of the rest of the book. That thought recalled to her mind the thought she had earlier, before Peter called, about the possibility of Max stealing the book.

She sighed and shook her head as she got out of bed. She wouldn't let herself entertain unfounded thoughts like that. She remembered the other two books in that little room off the wine cellar, and she resolved to ask Max if he would be interested in translating them, as well. Judging by the fact that they were not encased in custom-made Lucite boxes, her presumption was that they were neither as old nor as valuable. Still, the idea of entrusting Max with the task, if he was interested in it, helped her to not let her imagination, and Peter's trust issues, run away with her.

While she got dressed, Hayley made a mental note to find out what translation services cost, in case Max was interested. She didn't want to take advantage of him.

She smiled as she remembered his soft kiss the other evening. And his gentle voice. And the way he allowed her to decide about the goodnight kiss.

Then, there was Peter, the sensitive guy who became moody when talking about someone who had wronged him. Hayley didn't fault him for that. Based on the information he had, it was a valid complaint. But then, he wasn't above apologizing for 'spoiling the evening.' She liked a man who could utter a real apology without turning it around onto her.

She felt a little awkward, though. She had never been in the position of being attracted to two men at the same time, both of whom were interested in her, and both of whom knew each other. That situation, she found, came with a twinge of guilt. When she spent time with one of them, she felt almost like she was cheating on the other one.

She knew she would have to reconcile these feelings somehow. She had only known both of them for a few days, and was nowhere near being exclusive with either of them. But still, it felt awkward.

Hayley decided that she needed a distraction. She resolved that, after breakfast, she would go through some of the boxes in the basement. Having a plan of action helped to take her mind off the dilemma. A few albums of good music pumping through the house as she sorted would help even more.

§

Late in the morning, Hayley had the idea of dropping in on Max, to see how the rest of the book was coming along, and to see if he was available for some lunch. She didn't know what his class schedule was like, and she figured that if he wasn't available, she could always come back home, or go out by herself. But at least she could get an update on the book, and possibly a few more chapters to read.

And she liked the idea of surprising him.

Stotzheim University looked as if it had been designed as a chronological diorama. In fact, it wasn't by design, but by providence. The original buildings, beautiful nineteenth-century stone structures, stood with their backs against the Leine River on the west. Through the decades, as the university grew and more property was needed, it was gradually acquired and built eastward, the structures reflecting the architectural style of their day. By the time they reached the current eastern boundary, the buildings were sleek and modern.

The campus was tied together into a beautiful, cohesive unit by thoughtfully-designed tree-lined walkways and gardens, and Hayley was enjoying her walk in the sun-dappled tunnel formed by the trees arching overhead. It was still a few minutes before noon, and she felt like she could take her time.

Max's office and classroom were in one of the older buildings, and knowing him, she was sure he was glad of that. As she walked toward that building, looking at all the greenery around her, she looked down over a railing into a rose garden that was several steps below where she was. On one of the benches, she saw Max talking with another man.

To her surprise, her heart quickened a little when she saw him. She slowed her pace and watched him, appreciating his gestures, his posture, the way he filled out the greenish tweed blazer with brown suede elbow patches, even silly things like the shape of his head and his perpetually tousled hair. She thought she was being ridiculous, and she shook her head.

His back was to her, against the stone retaining wall that the railing was set in. Hayley was now almost directly above him, and now she saw what was in his hands. He was speaking quietly with this other person, showing him printouts of the book, *her* book. She recognized the crowded gothic lettering and the ornate illuminated drop caps at the beginning of each chapter.

She had almost called out to him, and now, she was glad she hadn't. She leaned against the rail and turned her head a little, trying to hear what was being said. She silently cursed the breeze that was causing a murmur in the foliage around her.

Then, she realized it didn't make any difference when she heard them conversing in German.

Max pointed to a few different areas on the printouts, and the other man nodded. Since she couldn't understand the words, she tried to decipher what their gestures might mean, but her efforts were wasted.

After a few minutes, the other man nodded, and they shook hands. Hayley followed the railing around to where the steps went downward into the garden. By the time she got down to the level of the rose garden, the other man was gone and Max was stuffing the papers into his briefcase.

"Hayley!" he said with surprise when he saw her. He stood up and nodded toward her.

"Hi, Max," she replied. "Who was that?" she asked.

"Oh," he said, glancing nervously over his shoulder, "that was Professor Weber." He was quick to change the subject. "I have wonderful news! I am almost finished with the translation. I only have a couple more chapters to go."

"That's great," Hayley said, trying not to sound as suspicious as she felt at the moment. Max was digging in his briefcase and pulled out a folder containing a small sheaf of papers.

"Perhaps we can get together tomorrow for dinner," he said. "I think I shall be finished by then, and we can relax and get to know each other." He sounded almost like a shy little boy.

"Sure," Hayley agreed, "that would be nice." Her feelings were conflicted, and she didn't know how to feel.

Max suddenly shook his head as he looked at her, as if he just realized something.

"Why are you here?"

"I just thought I'd drop by and see if you wanted to go get some lunch."

He smiled warmly at her, but then he looked quickly at his watch.

"I would love to," he said, "but I have a class in a few minutes." Hayley nodded.

"Okay," she replied, "I knew I was taking a chance. But I wanted to surprise you, and I figured I might at least get a few more chapters to read." She held up the folder in a triumphant gesture.

"It *was* a surprise. A very nice one. Perhaps we can get an early start tomorrow," Max suggested. "I could pick you up in the afternoon, and take you to see the *Georgengarten* before dinner."

"That would be very nice," Hayley smiled. "I'm looking forward to seeing it."

By the time they parted, Hayley felt silly for having been suspicious of him before. Why would he so diligently work at translating the book for her if he had some nefarious plan? In fact, all of this work was connecting him conspicuously to the book, leaving a ponderous paper trail of evidence.

She shook her head and decided that it was just another instance of Peter's suspicion rubbing off on to her.

§

"Oh my god, you look gorgeous!" Peter said after Hayley opened the door. She smiled and blushed, and she stepped to the side to allow him to come inside.

"Do you like opera?" he asked.

"I do," she replied, looking at Peter with an expression that could only be called cautiously hopeful.

"Great!" Peter replied, pumping his fist. "I had a feeling you might. I managed to snag us a couple of tickets for tonight."

"Peter, you're a college student!" Hayley protested. "You shouldn't be spending that kind of money on me."

"Don't get used to it," Peter smiled. "But I just felt like I owed you after last night."

"You don't owe me a thing."

"Okay, fine. I *wanted* to do it. Besides, I like opera, too. And the season is almost over, so we're just getting in under the wire."

"Well, thank you, Peter," Hayley said sincerely.

"Don't thank me yet. I've never heard of this opera, or the composer. I think it's a modern German production, and I have no idea what it's like."

"Still, that was very thoughtful." She looked down at what she was wearing. "And thank you for texting me about the dress code tonight."

"You really do look great."

"So do you!" Hayley said, trying not to be too obvious as she looked at him. He was dressed in a beautifully tailored black suit and white shirt. He wasn't wearing a tie, his open collar softening the formality of the ensemble. "I'm afraid I didn't bring an evening gown. I hope this will do."

She was wearing a black dress that she had brought just in case she had to go to anything having to do with her father. Two years after his death, she didn't think it was likely, but she had wanted to be prepared for anything. The dress was of a simple design, but it hugged the contours of her figure.

"It will do *very* nicely," Peter said, his voice a little ragged and breathy. Hayley suddenly felt very warm as his eyes slid up and down her body. "I'm going to have to fight all the other guys off of you!"

She rolled her eyes and shook her head, but that was just a pretense. She could feel the flush beginning right about where the scooped neck showed a little cleavage, and the heat climbed up her neck and face. She casually draped a crimson shawl over her shoulders, despite the lingering warmth of Peter's approving gaze.

§

Peter had finally been able to drive Hayley's car for more than five minutes at a time, although now, on the way back to Hayley's house, he seemed a little irritated at having to shift gears. Sitting down in the car, Hayley's hemline had risen, exposing several inches of thigh, and Peter's hand was resting there, caressing her leg when he didn't have to shift.

Dinner had been delicious. Peter took her to an Italian restaurant, and it was interesting to see how Germans interpreted the cuisine. Some of the dishes Hayley recognized, others were completely unfamiliar.

The warmth that she had begun to feel before they left her house continued in the restaurant as Peter's eyes were practically glued to her. She had to admit she was having a hard time taking her eyes off him, as well.

The opera was *L'Upupa und der Triumph der Sohnesliebe*, or *The Hoopoe and the Triumph of Filial Love*, by Hans Werner Henze, a contemporary German composer. Hayley was thankful for the English translation in the program so that she could follow the rather complex story, though she had to admit that it didn't leave any memorable melodies in her head.

In fact, one of the most memorable parts of the opera wasn't on the stage. It was when Peter shifted positions in his seat, and his hand brushed against her thigh. The surprise of his touch sent a tingle up her leg and she shivered. Peter noticed and interpreted that as a sign that she was cold, so he put his arm around her.

They had been touching each other in some form or fashion ever since then.

Peter drove through the open gate toward Hayley's house, and as he followed the long driveway around the house, he pressed the button on the remote that opened the garage door nearest the main part of the house. He pulled into the garage, shut off the engine and closed the garage door.

Without a word, they both opened their doors and got out of the car. Hayley, being closest to the door leading into the house, opened it and they silently went inside. In the kitchen, Peter took her hand and turned her around to face him. He backed her against the counter peninsula jutting into the kitchen, and he picked her up at the waist and sat her down on it.

He leaned in to kiss her, and Hayley wrapped her legs around him. As her legs tensed, she pulled him closer, and he kissed her with a renewed frenzy. During the course of the tangle of wet lips and tongues, Peter's hands caressed up and down her sides. He moved his right hand around to the front and cupped her breast, and she gasped and held her breath momentarily when his left hand pulled her hips forward tightly against him.

"Oh my god, Max," she said when she could speak again, "you feel so good!"

Peter stopped and pulled away from her. Hayley opened her eyes and looked at him, wondering why he had stopped.

"What's wrong?" she asked, seeing the expression on his face.

"You called me Max."

"Oh, Peter," Hayley breathed. "Did I really?" Peter nodded. She put a hand up to her face in embarrassment. "I'm so sorry," she whispered.

"It's alright," he muttered unconvincingly. "Maybe we're rushing it a little."

Hayley sighed despondently. Peter heard the sigh and looked at her, shaking his head.

"Hayley, it's okay," he managed to smile at her. "Really. We've got plenty of time."

She looked at him incredulously. Then, as her positive thinking took over, she smiled and nodded.

"You're right. I guess there's no rush."

Peter winked at her as he straightened his jacket, and he pulled his keys out of his pocket, twirling them once around his finger.

"But I'm not done with you, yet," he said blithely. He leaned forward and kissed her, then walked out of the kitchen. A few seconds later, she heard the front door open and close.

Chapter 24

Bergh von Hoffmann awoke early in the morning, before it was light. He didn't know what woke him, but he vaguely heard, in the distance, a tune that pulled at him. Without knowing why, he got out of bed and reached for his crutches. No one else was up yet, and he saw nobody as he made his way down the stairs and out the front door.

Swinging along on his crutches, he followed the notes, a tune that drew him along. Something inside him responded to the melody and, as if he had no choice, he followed it. He reached the gates of the town and saw, far ahead of him, illuminated hazily by the dimly approaching dawn, other children of Hamelin. They seemed to be pulled along by the melody, as well.

Bergh struggled to keep up, but they were so far ahead of him. He couldn't catch up, let alone keep up. The tune was a happy one, and many of the children were dancing to it as they followed. Yet the tune also had notes of longing that drew Bergh after it. He kept following as quickly as he could, finally reaching the gates at the other end of town.

As he got there, he saw the other children dancing along to the tune, trampling the grass along the edge of a cliff that climbed up the hill, and filing into a cave. Bergh struggled to reach them, because what he and they heard was so wonderful, so compelling, that they had no choice.

Panting from the exertion, tears filled Bergh's eyes as he watched the last child disappear into the cave as the piper stood there at the entrance, playing the melody that burned his heart and pulled him along. He was still so far behind, he knew he could never catch up.

Suddenly, the piper played a distinctive trill on the flute, and the ground began to shake. The melody stopped, as did the pull on Bergh's heart. He watched in horror as rocks began to fall, sealing the entrance to the cave. Emotionally and physically exhausted, Bergh saw a shaft of early morning sunlight illuminate the piper's face. The man smiled coldly, then turned and walked away.

§

Bewildered, Bergh wandered slowly back through town. Dawn was casting long shadows across the street as Mayor Hildebrandt emerged from one of them.

"Young man," he said, "are you alright?"

Bergh looked at him with confusion etched on his face.

"You're young Master von Hoffmann, aren't you?" the Mayor said as the boy came closer.

"They're all gone," Bergh said.

"Who are all gone?" Bergh looked up at him, and a tear found its way out of his eye and down his cheek. Before he said another word, a door opened nearby.

"Otto?" called a woman. She came into the street looking both directions. When she saw the Mayor, she walked over to him. "My Otto is gone," she said.

Mayor Hildebrandt looked down at Bergh, as he heard another set of footsteps approaching.

"I can't find Giselle."

Within a few moments, they were joined by more parents looking in vain for their children. Mayor Hildebrandt knelt down in front of Bergh.

"Son, what can you tell us?"

"The piper," Bergh said, his words coming out in sobs, "he played a tune on his pipe and we had to follow. They're sealed in a cave now, probably dead."

The Mayor frowned, trying to understand.

"Alright, calm down. Tell me what happened."

Bergh took a deep breath and roughly wiped his eyes.

"I heard a song that I had to follow. It was the piper, the man that led the rats out of Hamelin. He was playing the song, and all the children of the town were following him.

"I was trying to follow. I couldn't help it. But I couldn't catch up with them. Then, I saw him lead them into a cave outside of town. When he stopped playing, a rockslide sealed up the cave. All the children are in there, and they can't get out."

The Mayor understood Bergh's words, but the story was too fantastic. How could something like that be true? Yet a man ridding their down of rats with his flute was just as fantastic.

"Can you show me where the children are?" he asked. Wiping fresh tears away, Bergh nodded.

As if Bergh were the piper himself, he led a growing crowd of parents out of town, finally coming to a stop at the base of the hill that he hadn't been able to climb fast enough. They could see the path that all the children had trampled through the grass and weeds along the edge of the cliff. They could see what had been a cave, now sealed up with rocks, the freshly-disturbed dirt still damp on them.

A couple of the men clambered up the path and started trying to pull the rocks out of the mouth of the cave. They were wedged tightly and couldn't be budged, almost as if fortified by the magic of the piper's flute.

Suddenly, a tune sounded around them, a melody so awash with resignation and melancholia that tears came instantly to the eyes of the listeners. Mayor Hildebrandt wiped his eyes and turned to see the piper up on the hill, a few meters from the cave.

Then, through her sobs, one of the women screamed. Mayor Hildebrandt saw one of the men up at the cave move toward the edge of the cliff and step off. Moments later, his companion followed him over.

"Please, sir," the Mayor cried, "these people have done nothing to you."

The piper stopped playing and, almost instantaneously, the melancholy feeling ended, except for the two women who rushed down toward the river where their wailing intensified. Those remaining looked confused, as if they didn't know what had happened.

"These people have cheated me of the payment that is rightfully mine," the piper replied, "the payment that they agreed to."

"It was not they who cheated you," shouted the Mayor. "They all paid their share. Only one man was responsible for this."

"Who is this man?" someone in the crowd asked.

The Mayor glanced around almost as if he were afraid to say. But as he looked around, he heard the clomping of horse hooves as Reynold rode up toward them.

"I'm looking for my son," he said. "Is he up here?"

"He is," Mayor Hildebrandt replied through clenched teeth. "But the rest of the children of the town are gone because of you."

"Because of me?" von Hoffmann replied contemptuously. "What are you talking about?"

"You didn't pay your share to the piper, and now he has drawn the children away. They've been swallowed up in the mountain. All our children are gone, probably dead," a few gasps sounded from the crowd, joining the wailing down by the river, "and two of our men are dead because of your arrogance and greed!"

"Watch yourself, Mayor," von Hoffmann said in an ominously quiet, warning voice. "You forget who you're speaking to."

"I forget nothing. Pay your share before we lose any more."

"As I told you last night, I did not agree to this arrangement. And my son was not taken, so why should I pay money to this stranger?"

As the grumbling in the crowd behind him grew louder, the Mayor stepped closer to von Hoffmann.

"You may feel no compunction to pay because of these people," Mayor Hildebrandt said quietly, his voice seething with anger, "but perhaps you will for your own self-preservation."

"You're speaking nonsense again, Mayor," von Hoffmann replied haughtily.

"I am making perfect sense." By now, Mayor Hildebrandt was standing next to von Hoffmann and lowered his voice. "What if word should get to the Duke that you have been spending time with his wife? Perhaps you might not be quite so arrogant then."

The expression on von Hoffmann's face was so drenched in malice that, for a moment, Mayor Hildebrandt wondered if he had gone too far.

"You wouldn't," von Hoffmann sneered, looking down his nose at the Mayor.

Mayor Hildebrandt glanced over his shoulder toward the others. Whatever fondness any of them might have remotely felt for von Hoffmann before had plummeted when they heard that he had not paid his share to the piper.

"Perhaps if more people knew about it," the Mayor said, raising his voice a little as a threat.

"Alright," von Hoffmann finally said, his eyes burning with hatred. He pulled a money bag from inside his cloak and counted out several gold coins, dropping them bitterly into the Mayor's outstretched hands.

"We have your money," Mayor Hildebrandt said, turning instantly toward the piper who had been watching the proceedings. "Please return our children!"

The piper walked cautiously down the hillside toward the Mayor, taking the money from him. He counted the coins, then deposited them in the bag with the rest of the money. He looked at Mayor Hildebrandt for a few moments, then lifted his head decisively.

"I must contemplate for a while."

The Mayor and others in the crowd behind him felt a sudden feeling of foreboding.

"What is there to contemplate?" the Mayor asked. "You have your money. Return our children!"

"I will meet you back here at noon," the piper replied. Then, he turned and climbed back up the hillside, disappearing into the forest.

Chapter 25

The *Georgengarten* began in 1726 as four rows of lime trees. Stretching a little over a mile long, it connected the city of Hannover with the palace and gardens of *Herrenhausen*.

Early in the nineteenth century, the gardens were enlarged by King George III, King of Hannover. *Herrenhausen* Palace, at the time, was the official summer residence of King George who, coincidentally, was the same King George who ruled over Great Britain and Ireland.

Hayley was surprised to learn of this connection between Britain and Germany. She was also surprised to note that the lime trees that Max spoke of were not the kind that grew limes, but were what she knew as linden trees.

And they were in bloom! Hayley loved the smell of linden blossoms. With this many of them in bloom, the aroma was almost overpowering. And with the hundreds of trees lining the wide avenue all bearing the small, fragrant white flowers, the effect was magical.

Max was very knowledgeable about the gardens, both the botany and the history. *Herrenhausen* Palace, for instance, had been extensively damaged during the bombing in 1943, during World War II. It wasn't until 2009 that it was decided to rebuild the palace, and it was opened in 2013, just under seventy years after the bombing.

In what was either a practical move or a sly maneuver, Max took Hayley's hand and drew her off that main avenue onto a smaller path that branched off to the west. They strolled over a lovely bridge with a green scrolled ironwork railing that crossed what looked like a river, but Hayley suspected was part of a network of man-made waterways designed in the garden.

Max was still holding her hand when they reached the *Leibniztempel*, a round classical-styled pavilion with twelve smooth Ionic columns. It served as a monument to polymath Gottfried Wilhelm Leibniz who died in 1716. They climbed the four shallow steps where the bust of Leibniz stood on a pedestal in the center of the monument. Turning, they looked eastward across the water reflecting the lush greenery of the trees. It was a perfect day, and Hayley was moved by her surroundings, and by Max's attention.

On the grass near the water, an older couple were enjoying a picnic, and they had brought a boom box with them. Hayley was surprised to hear *In the Mood* by Glenn Miller playing, and it recalled to her mind the scene in the movie *The Glenn Miller Story* where he and his orchestra were playing this song to an audience of English servicemen.

While they were playing, a Nazi buzz bomb could be heard flying in, and a few people began running for cover. The musicians, though, continued playing while their die-hard fans stayed to listen. The bomb eventually exploded somewhere off-screen, teaching the valuable lesson that, apparently, uninterrupted music is more important than life.

But it was a fun scene. At least those who were likely killed by the bomb were elsewhere in the city, not any of these enjoying the music.

Max, still holding Hayley's hand, impulsively turned her around and began doing a basic foxtrot with her to the music. Hayley was, at first, shocked, then delighted as they danced the circular floor around Leibniz.

It had been a while since she had done any serious dancing, but it quickly came back to her. Max didn't seem to be an expert by any means, so she was able to keep up with him.

When the song ended, Max held Hayley close, apparently hoping that a slow song would be next. To his dismay, Benny Goodman's *Sing, Sing, Sing (With a Swing)* began, starting with Gene Krupa's frantic drumming.

Feeling his arms around her, and seeing his face, Hayley recognized what Max had hoped for, and a compassionate smile settled on her face. She felt his hands start to loosen, and in an instant, she held his hand tighter, closed her eyes and concentrated. She started swaying back and forth on every other beat of the song, ignoring the frenetic tempo. She heard Max chuckle, and he started swaying with her. They found the slower rhythm embedded in the song and slow-danced their way around the pavilion while Benny Goodman's orchestra belted out the music.

By the time the almost nine minute song finally ended, Hayley and Max both seemed reluctant to let the other go. They stood there in the pavilion holding each other. Hayley turned her face up toward Max and, in contrast with a few nights ago, he immediately pressed his lips against hers.

Hayley put an arm around his neck, passionately returning his kiss and holding him tightly. If she had thought about it, she would have been certain that what she was feeling wasn't just the frustrated sexual tension spilling over from last night with Peter. She truly was attracted to Max. Max was about ten years older than Peter, and that maturity meant something to Hayley.

But she wasn't thinking about that. She was just feeling the heat of Max's ardor, and the sensitivity of his growing attachment to her. She was feeling that attachment, herself.

Peter did cross her mind as she was lip-locked with Max, but only as a young and exciting attraction, a "passing fancy," one that, she realized, was quickly being replaced with the deeper affection that was growing in her for Max. Her thoughts of Peter were immediately pushed aside as Max, in his romantic fervor, brought his hands up and placed one on each side of her face, as if he needed to still be in contact with her when their lips parted.

He gazed deeply into her eyes, and Hayley felt tears in hers as she saw the affection that she had been feeling being returned.

Neither of them even realized that the slow song that Max had hoped for earlier was now playing, as Tommy Dorsey's *I'm Getting Sentimental Over You* played on the boom box.

§

"I was surprised to hear American swing music playing back there," Hayley said as they walked back under the linden trees, their arms around each other's waists. "It reminded me of a movie several years ago, *Swing Kids*, about young people in Nazi Germany who were so into American and English music and dance that the Nazis considered them a threat. But I just figured that was a fictional concept someone came up with to make a dance movie."

"Oh, it was real," Max confirmed. "They were known as Schlurfs. Their opposition to the Nazis was not based on a political stance, but just the typical tendency of youth to oppose conformity and adult regulation. They had no idea, yet, of the danger that existed in the Nazis. To them, it was just a game, a simple teenage rebellion."

They walked silently for a while. It was such a lovely, lazy afternoon, Hayley's thoughts drifted, from Nazi Germany to the story of the Pied Piper of Hamelin, to a few friends and her mother, people she missed back home, to the new friends she had made here.

She was brought back by the scent of the linden flowers wafting around her, and by a breeze that sent countless delicate white blossoms falling around them like snow. It was a perfect moment, and she looked up at Max. He felt her move, and he looked down at her and smiled.

131

He leaned in for another brief kiss, then they continued on their way, holding each other a little tighter.

§

Dinner was very nice, at a romantic French restaurant. Hayley and Max talked easily and comfortably for well over an hour, while holding hands across the table before their dinner came, then while casually enjoying their food and wine.

In Hayley's mind, the time was marred only once when she made the careless mistake of mentioning the opera that Peter had taken her to the evening before, and she saw that darkness pass across his face. It was fleeting, and Max recovered quickly, but Hayley was determined to be more careful.

As Hayley finished her chocolate mousse, she pushed the dish away a bit and looked at Max.

"We've been talking for hours now," she said, "and we haven't even said anything about my book. Were you able to finish it?"

"I did," he nodded. "It is out in the trunk of my car, along with the last two chapters. You can have it back tonight."

"Wonderful!" Hayley said, anxious to see how the story ends. "That didn't take long at all."

"No, it is a fairly small book, and the print is rather large." Then, his eyes sparkled with excitement like they had when she first showed him the book Monday morning. "But it was a lot of fun!"

"That's great," Hayley said. "I have a couple of other old books. Maybe if you're interested," she shrugged and waved her hand. "But we can talk about that another time."

"Perhaps," Max nodded.

Having finished his *crème brûlée,* he reached across the table and took her hand in his. He held it for a few moments, gazing at its delicate lines. He caressed the back of it with his thumb, until Hayley lifted it and intertwined her fingers with his. Max smiled. Hayley did too, admiring how natural it felt, how nicely their hands fit together, how comfortable she felt in his presence.

Against her will, her thoughts went back to the previous evening with Peter. She felt almost ashamed to be thinking about that now when she was with Max. That heat, that raw passion had been exciting, but she didn't know if there was anything of substance beyond it.

With Max, the passion was there, too, as he had demonstrated at the *Leibniztempel*. But there was also the romanticism that had prompted the whole afternoon and evening. There was his quiet thoughtfulness, which was exhibited in so many ways. And there was the ardent attraction that he obviously felt for her, and wasn't afraid to display in public.

Then, there was the fact that Hayley felt that attraction, as well. The easy comfort she felt when she was with Max was so pleasant.

As they finished in the restaurant and made their way outside to Max's car, they were still holding hands, but Max's grip seemed tentative. Hayley looked at him and saw that the shy little boy was back. He looked as if he wanted to say something, but didn't know quite how.

He opened the door for her and she got in. He went around to his side and settled behind the wheel, but he didn't start the car right away.

"What is it, Max?" Hayley prompted.

He hesitated a moment longer as he looked at her.

"Would you like to come over to my place?" he finally asked quietly.

Hayley smiled and thought for a few moments, looking down at her hands folded in her lap as she nervously dug at her cuticles. The thoughts that had been tumbling around in her head that evening were tangled up too tightly. She couldn't make sense of them yet. Finally, she looked up at Max.

"I'd like to," she said, "but not tonight."

Chapter 26

Ely sat on the stool which had become her usual place when Cort was working. She enjoyed watching him work, seeing how a creative mind realized its imaginings. And it was even more pleasant now without the rats crawling all over the place.

Lately, though, she had been watching Cort with a new kind of interest. After their discussion a couple of days before in which she realized that her past didn't matter to him, she was seeing him in a new light.

His attraction to her was obvious. She had seen that most of her life from men. But the thought that there could be something deeper, something stronger, was a new idea to her. That she might be feeling something similar was an even stranger concept. And the more she thought about it, the more closely she watched Cort, the greater her own attraction to him grew.

But as the idea took root, the more remote a normal life with him seemed. How could it be possible? She was known as a prostitute. People had seen her in and around the town for years. Cort had been a mighty, respected warrior and was now a respectable tradesman. The idea of him becoming united to someone like her was just unheard of.

Her ponderings were interrupted when she heard someone approaching. She got up to go inside, but then she recognized the sound. She heard the distinctive step and swish, and she knew that Bergh was coming on his crutches.

Cort glanced up at her when she rose, and she motioned toward the gate in the wall of his courtyard just as Bergh showed up there. They both knew right away, though, that something was not right. He looked up at both of them, and his eyes filled with tears.

"Bergh," Cort said, "what's wrong?" He pulled the other stool over for him and Bergh lowered himself onto it.

Bergh hesitated, his eyes cast downward, as if he had something difficult to say, but Cort and Ely waited patiently for him. Finally, he looked up at them and spoke.

"My father is a bad man."

Cort and Ely looked at each other. They were both familiar with von Hoffmann, and knew that Bergh's assessment was correct, but rather than openly agree with him, they waited.

"My father is the reason why the children are gone."

"What?" Ely asked, her face contorted in a frown. "What children?"

Bergh looked back and forth at both of them, surprised that they knew nothing about it.

"The children of Hamelin. You haven't heard?" They both shook their heads. "The piper, the man that led the rats away yesterday, led all the children of Hamelin away this morning and into a cave, and sealed the entrance with rocks."

"Why would he do that?" Cort asked.

"Because my father refused to pay his share of the price," Bergh said, his eyes refilling. His voice cracked as he continued. "He didn't pay until the Mayor threatened him in some way. I'm ashamed to be his son."

Cort grasped the boy's shoulder sympathetically. Ely leaned forward.

"What about the children?" she asked. "How did he take them?"

"I don't know," Bergh replied, remembering the tune. "He played some kind of music on his flute that made us want to follow him. It woke me up this morning, and I had to go. I can't describe it. I just couldn't help it." He roughly wiped the tears from his eyes and kicked his crutches. "But I couldn't keep up."

"And they're sealed up in a cave?" Cort prodded. Bergh nodded.

"My father finally paid when the other parents and the Mayor got angry at him. But the piper didn't let the children go. The Mayor thinks they may be dead. The piper said to meet him back there at noon."

"Where?"

"That cave above the river," Bergh said, pointing, "not far from here."

Cort looked up at Ely.

"I have to go."

Ely nodded as Bergh pushed himself up on his crutches.

"I'll show you where," he said.

§

Cort struggled with the rocks sealing the cave as he thought about Bergh's fanciful story concerning this piper. The rocks were wedged so tightly together, he began wondering if the magic this piper used was at work on the rocks as well. He was beginning to lose hope that he would be able to dislodge any of them.

Finally, he felt the stone begin to loosen a little, and rocking it back and forth, he managed to pull it free. As the stone came loose, he pushed it to the side where it crashed to the ground on his left, tumbling over the cliff and rolling into the river below.

He grasped the stone next to the indentation left by the one he had just removed when he felt a hand on his shoulder. He turned to see Abelard, the baker. Cort purchased bread from him frequently. He knew that Abelard and his wife had a young daughter, and she was likely sealed up in the cave with the others.

"I'm glad you're here," Abelard said. "I didn't want to wait for this piper."

He had a pickaxe in his hand, and he started to swing it, but Cort stopped him.

"We should start up high," he explained. "I don't want to undermine the rocks and have them collapse on us, or worse, on the children in the cave."

"Of course," Abelard nodded, "good idea." The anxiety showing in his eyes was obvious, but he tried to keep it at bay, to focus his attention on the goal. He handed the pickaxe to Cort to try to loosen the rock he had just started on, as a few other men began arriving to help.

Cort wedged the point of the pickaxe between that stone and the one next to it, and pushing the handle, he was able to dislodge it. He pushed it to the side as he had the previous one, and he turned an encouraging smile toward Abelard.

But Abelard wasn't there. Cort turned and looked around just as Abelard stepped off the cliff, his body crashing onto the rocks below. Unable to believe his eyes, Cort saw another person step off the cliff after him. He tossed the pickaxe down as others made their way toward the edge of the cliff. The intense sadness showing on their faces was almost tangible.

Cort moved between them and the cliff, his arms stretched out at his side, blocking them, physically pushing some of them back. Just then, he saw over their heads, the man that Bergh had described. The piper was playing his flute, and the people continued trying to push toward the cliff.

"Please, stop!" Cort shouted. "These people just want their children!"

The piper stopped playing and, almost instantaneously, the men stopped pushing against Cort. They all looked confused, milling about as if they were lost.

"I told all of you to meet me back here at noon and I would give my answer. I did not instruct you to try to dig them out yourself."

But the man was too far away for Cort to understand.

"I'm sorry," Cort said, moving closer to him, while guiding the people away from the edge of the cliff, "I am deaf. I must see your mouth."

"Ah," the piper sneered, "that explains why you were immune to my melancholy song."

"As I told you, piper," shouted Mayor Hildebrandt as he started up the path, "it was Baron von Hoffmann who cheated you. And even he has paid now. Please, if the children are still alive, return them to their parents!"

"The people of this town seem to have difficulty following simple instructions," the piper said. "That will cost you. My price has doubled." An appalled gasp rose from the growing crowd.

"Doubled? That is outrageous!" the Mayor protested. "We could barely scrape together one thousand guilders."

"Well, perhaps it's better this way," the piper hissed acerbically. "Children can be such demanding, messy little creatures. And they're so expensive to take care of."

"Please," Cort said, trying to keep his voice level, "these poor people just want their children back."

The piper raised the flute to his lips and began playing a slow, droning tune. Unable to hear the melody, Cort anxiously turned and looked at the men behind him, but rather than jumping off the cliff, everyone started submissively filing down the path toward their homes. The piper stopped playing long enough to deliver one last retort.

"You know the terms, and you know where to find me. I shall be here waiting for my payment."

A few of the men turned angrily toward him, but before they could take more than a couple of steps, the piper began his tune again, and they continued their passive march toward their homes.

Chapter 27

The book lay, sealed in its Lucite case, on the kitchen counter where Hayley had left it when Max dropped her off the night before. Just inches away from where Peter had sat her down the night before that and started the abbreviated lovemaking session.

Sitting on one of the stools at the counter, she idly fingered the case, deep in thought. Whenever she could get herself motivated, she'd take it down to the basement and put it back in its place in the little room of antiquities in the wine cellar. For now, she just felt mentally and emotionally lethargic.

She had decided to keep to herself on Sunday. Her thoughts and emotions were a little overwhelming, and she felt as if she needed the time alone to process everything. Despite invitations from both Max and Peter, she stayed at home all day.

While she was flattered by their attention, she was perturbed by the position it put her in. She had always been a fiercely loyal person, with friends and lovers. Dating two men at the same time who were both so interested in her made her feel disloyal to both of them. She knew that, inevitably, somebody was going to get hurt, and that she was going to be the one to do it.

Peter, the more persistent of the two, called her again that evening. During their brief conversation, Hayley told him that Max had finished the translation and had given her back the book. Peter was happy to hear that, and relieved that his fears about Max had not panned out. He said he had a long stretch between classes the next day and wondered if Hayley wanted to get together for an early lunch. She accepted. By then, she knew what she was going to do.

§

Being early, the restaurant they had chosen wasn't busy. Hayley and Peter were seated and served right away. They made quick work of ordering, and then engaged in a little awkward small talk.

Or, at least, it was awkward for Hayley.

"So, Professor Schiller finished translating your book, huh?" Peter asked, moving on to an actual topic of conversation.

"Yes, I have the book back in my possession, so you can calm your suspicions about him." As she was saying it, she realized that it sounded almost as if she was scolding him, so she tried to soften it with a smile.

"That's great," Peter replied. "Have you finished reading it yet?"

"Not quite. I still have a couple of chapters to go."

"Well, I'm glad you have it back now," Peter said. He looked at her quizzically, as if he suspected that something was amiss. Hayley had never been very good at hiding her emotions, so she decided that she should just spill it.

"Peter, I guess I'm kind of old-fashioned. I'm not . . ." she thought for a moment, "promiscuous, for lack of a better word. I don't feel right dating both you and Max.

"I know where you and I were headed the other night and, well," she blushed, "it was *really* nice. But frankly, I felt like I was being unfaithful to Max. Then, when Max kissed me, I felt like I was cheating on you. I don't like that feeling."

She paused when she saw the look on Peter's face.

"Hayley, I—" he started. He studied his fork for a moment, then looked up at her. "I like you a lot."

"And I like you, too," Hayley nodded.

"I thought we were having fun."

"It *was* fun," she agreed. "I had a great time with you."

"Then why not continue and see where it goes?"

"Because I'm having a great time with Max, too. And I can't keep feeling torn, wanting you both, and feeling like

I'm being unfaithful to both of you. That's not fair to any of us."

"I didn't know you were looking for something serious."

"I wasn't."

She remembered all the mental back-and-forth she did the day before. She had almost envied people who could date multiple people at the same time and keep it all casual. But she realized that, to her, sex was more serious than that.

"So, you're just cutting us both loose?"

Hayley looked at Peter, and she felt the tears come, as she knew they would. She wiped them away and shook her head.

"No," she said in barely a whisper.

§

If Hayley thought it was awkward before, the rest of their time together was downright ungainly. To his credit, Peter respected her decision and didn't beg or complain. But there were long intervals of uncomfortable silence during their lunch. She didn't think there were twenty words spoken between them after that.

She watched Peter drive away, back toward the university, and she got in her car, wiping yet another tear from her eye, and started toward home.

She couldn't help wondering if she had made the right decision. Peter was young and passionate, spontaneous and exciting. But rather than second-guessing herself, she remembered her thought processes of the day before.

Hayley knew that she wasn't as spontaneous and exciting as she had been back in college. Back then, it wasn't uncommon for her to stay up all night with her friends, or with a particular guy, doing crazy things, being spontaneous, young.

She was still young, but she had become responsible. She had settled into daily routines, habits and customs that

142

she liked, that made her feel comfortable. While her time with Peter had been fun and exciting, she knew she couldn't live like that regularly.

Max, on the other hand, was balanced and steady. He could certainly be passionate, but his predominant qualities of tranquility and calm were more compatible with her lifestyle now. She nodded, certain that her decision had been the right one.

She sighed heavily as she drove into her garage and parked the car. As the garage door cranked back down, she got out of the car and went into the house.

She sighed and tossed her purse on the counter as she plopped down on one of the stools. She hated the feeling of dumping someone, almost as much as she hated the feeling of being dumped. If Peter had been a hateful, abusive man, it would be different. But he wasn't. He was a sweet, thoughtful guy, handsome, passionate, romantic.

No wonder she dumped him!

She put her elbows on the counter and buried her face in her hands. A moment later, she lifted her head, a frown on her face. She looked around, her eyes scanning the kitchen. Something was tickling her brain, but she couldn't figure out what it was.

Hayley looked at her purse, lying there on the counter. And then, she realized what it was.

She got up and went downstairs. She had been tired and absent-minded yesterday, but she didn't remember taking the book back down to its room as she had resolved.

Entering the wine cellar, she went back to the corner in the rear, disconnected the last rack and swung it out, and opened the door behind it. She flipped on the switch and the dim light came to life, and just as she suspected, the book was not on the shelf.

So, why wasn't it on the kitchen counter where she knew she left it? Maybe, as preoccupied as she had been yesterday, she took it upstairs to her bedroom with the rest of the translated chapters.

However, after a quick run up the stairs, she saw the papers on her bedside table, but no book.

She began making a frantic search of her house. As she was doing that, she heard Peter's suspicions in her head about Max. About him stealing Peter's work and publishing it as his own. And she saw Max sitting on that bench with another man, showing him photocopies of the pages of her book.

She remembered how she had talked herself out of suspecting Max, that he was creating a paper trail from the book to himself. Now, she saw that it was a perfect ruse. All that work he put into translating the book for her, why would he do that if it was all going to point right back to him? Besides, he had the book, and he gave it back to her. She brought it home and had it back in her possession. That pretty much severed the paper trail.

Having visited every room in the house that she had been in during the last few days, she knew the book was gone. While she was breaking up with Peter, Max had stolen the book. She stormed back down the stairs and through the kitchen, grabbing her purse on the way through.

Chapter 28

Ely wandered aimlessly from Cort's cottage to the courtyard, to her sleeping quarters in his shed and back. She was distressed by Bergh's wild tale about this piper, and about the children of the town. If it was true, how frightened and worried the parents must be!

She wiped another tear from her eye, as she had numerous times already. She wanted a child of her own, but she knew it could not be. A pregnant prostitute was not a profitable one. When she had become pregnant a few years before, she had drunk a concoction designed to end the pregnancy. The solution was effective, but it had made her quite ill for several days.

She eventually recovered, but the solution was never needed again.

Her dream of a 'normal life' had always included a husband and children. Apparently, her dream, if it could be realized at all, was, at best, only halfway accessible.

With a heavy sigh, she sat down on her stool outside the door of the cottage. The emotions dredged up by Bergh's story, and by her empathy for the people of the town, were too much to bear. She buried her face in her hands and she cried.

After a few moments, she stopped and held her breath when a sound carried on the breeze caught her ear. She turned her head slightly to try to hear it again, and she waited. There it was again, the sound of a woman screaming.

Ely wiped her eyes and stood up, going out of the courtyard and venturing cautiously toward the front of the wall, where she risked being seen by others. She peeked around the corner and saw a scene that was familiar to her, but from a different point of view.

A couple of cottages away, a girl was being held down on the ground by two men. And there, kneeling between her legs, Ely saw Hans, the man who had raped her a few weeks before. The overwhelming sadness that Ely had felt earlier was now replaced by anger and righteous indignation.

But she knew she could do nothing for that poor girl unarmed. She quickly ran back into the courtyard, looking for something she could use to defend the girl and herself. Cort's carpentry tools were strewn about where he left them after Bergh told them about the piper. But they were small and would be ineffectual in a fight.

Then, she saw Cort's axe standing against the wall. How many times had she watched him swing that axe into a log, insert a wedge, then use the back of the axe head to hammer that wedge deeper, finally splitting from the log a piece of usable lumber? The axe head was heavy, the blade sharp.

Ely had a softer object in mind than an oak log.

Trembling with anger and fear, she grabbed the axe and scrambled out of the courtyard, running toward the girl and her trio of attackers. Kneeling between her legs, Hans had opened his codpiece and was inching forward. The girl was lying still, likely pummeled into submission as Ely had been.

Ely ran quickly but quietly. Her heart was pounding, remembering being raped a few weeks ago, while feeling for the poor girl who was about to endure the same thing now.

Hans lifted the girl's skirt, impatiently yanking aside the undergarments, and he moved forward on his knees. The attention of his two companions was focused down on the girl, so they didn't notice Ely's rapid approach until the last moment.

Hans leaned forward, supporting himself on his right hand, his left hand unseen down below, when Ely swung the axe. Her momentum added to the force as the blade buried itself deep in his back, severing his spine. The sudden inertia she encountered with his body helped her to stop her forward momentum.

She was aware of a momentary grunt being forced through Hans' throat, and he collapsed on top of the girl. In an immediate thought for their victim's well-being, Ely yanked the axe back toward herself, pulling the body off and away from the girl. The axe came free from the corpse, and she hefted it, the blade dripping with Hans' blood.

An expression of horror suffused the faces of Hans' companions, and with a brief look at the axe-wielding fury, they jumped up and ran away, nearly colliding with a shocked older couple approaching. As they looked toward Ely and the crying girl on the ground, the startled couple immediately ran toward them.

"Emelyne!" shouted the woman. The girl was dazed, her face bloodied and bruised, and hearing her name, she looked around. She pushed herself weakly up on her elbows. Ely knelt down and pulled Emelyne's skirt back down, and the girl smiled appreciatively at her, until she felt the pain on her face.

The woman knelt down beside Emelyne, touching her gingerly in fear of hurting her more. Ely stood up and backed away, wanting to allow them their privacy. Her heart was hammering in her chest, her breaths coming in ragged gasps, as she tried to recover from the momentary frenzy.

The man looked down at his daughter and at the bloody corpse beside her, then looked across at Ely.

"Young man," he started, but then he realized his mistake and seemed embarrassed. "Oh, miss," he stammered, "we, uh, we owe you a debt of gratitude."

"You don't owe me anything," Ely shook her head, trying to slow her breathing. "I'm only sorry I let his partners get away."

"No need to worry about that," he replied grimly. "I saw them. I know who they are."

Unable to hold herself up any longer, the axe slipped from her fingers, and Ely collapsed backward, the sky spinning above her.

Chapter 29

Max's classroom was empty when Hayley walked past, so she went straight to his office. She was seething by the time she pushed his door open, slamming it hard against the wall behind it.

"Alright, you son of a bitch, I want my book ba—"

Max looked up at her from the floor where he knelt down, brushing broken glass into a dust pan. Hayley looked around at Max's office, her unfinished statement ending with a long exhalation. His office had been demolished.

Books were scattered about, many of them ripped up, the pages scattered. The laptop computer on his desk had been smashed against the corner of his desk, leaving the computer broken and misshapen. Glass cabinet fronts were shattered. Folders and their contents had been ripped from the file cabinet and thrown around the office, and the file cabinet itself was tipped over on its side, one of the open drawers bent at an odd angle on its tracks. Every drawer had been pulled out of his desk and emptied on the desk top or on the floor.

"Oh my god, Max," Hayley said, her own anger over the missing book temporarily dissipating as she looked around at the savagery that had been vented on Max's office. "What happened?"

"Somebody broke in and ransacked my office," Max replied quietly, in a matter-of-fact tone.

"Sorry," Hayley replied, nodding her head. "Of course, I can see that."

"The police just left a little while ago and let me start cleaning up." He dumped the dust pan into a small trash can and stood up.

"Any leads on who did this, and why?"

"Not officially, but I think they were looking for your book. When they did not find it, they just became angry and smashed everything." Then, he looked at her straight on, as if just realizing something. "You said you want your book back?"

Hayley sighed.

"I'm sorry, Max. Somebody stole the book, and I'm afraid I suspected you."

"Me? Why?"

Hayley shook her head and looked around the ruins as she thought about her reasons.

"Okay," she finally said, picking up a couple of books at her feet, "I promised Peter I wouldn't be the one to tell you, but under the circumstances —"

"Peter?"

"Peter was suspicious of you because he said that you copied some of his work and published it as your own." Max frowned as if trying to understand. "I told him that, if that is what actually happened, you probably didn't even remember that it had come from someone else, and that you would likely be horrified to learn that you had copied someone else's work."

Max was still looking at her with his mouth open and a look of disbelief on his face.

"Peter accused me of this?" he asked, his accent becoming a little more prominent the more upset he became.

"He did," Hayley replied quietly, hoping she had done the right thing in telling him.

Max sighed heavily, angrily, and he righted the chair in front of his desk which was lying on its side.

"Have a seat," he said. His desk chair was still upright, but it was covered with papers and other items that had been in his desk drawers. He brushed it off and sat down. Hayley sat in the chair in front of his desk, the one she had sat in when she first met him. Was it really just a week ago?

"I met Peter last year when he enrolled in my *Deutschland im Mittelalter* class." He immediately shook his head and translated, "Germany in the Middle Ages. Right away, his knowledge and understanding of German history became apparent, as did his, I think you Americans call it work ethic.

"He was a hard worker, diligently applied himself to every assignment. When Henry, my assistant, disappeared, I decided to appoint Peter as my new assistant."

"Wait," Hayley interrupted, "your assistant disappeared?"

"Yes, one day, Henry did not show up for class. I never saw him again after that. There was an investigation, but to my knowledge, nothing was ever resolved. I believe the case is still open."

"Okay," Hayley prompted, getting back to the original topic, "so Peter is now your assistant."

"Yes. He is a good assistant. His knowledge of certain topics actually rivals mine. He is always agreeable to taking charge of a class when I ask him to.

"But, in time, as I was reading one of his papers, I came across something that was familiar. My memory was vague. I could not quite recall where I remembered it from. I spent several hours researching, but I found it, a journal that a professor had published a few years before.

"For Peter's paper, he did not 'copy and paste.' It was not word for word, but the arguments and conclusions were quite similar. Still, it was different enough that I was willing to dismiss it as a coincidence, an example of two people in the same field developing the same line of thought.

"But then it happened again. And again, it was obscure enough that it took me some time to find the original, and again, the wording, the phraseology was different. Some of the points were even in a different order, and Peter developed his conclusions based on that different order. And they still worked.

"So, again, I let it pass.

"When it happened a third time, I approached him about it. I presented his work and the original works that it appeared he had copied.

"He explained it as I had myself just now. He pointed out all the differences between the originals and the 'copies,' and how his conclusions came by different routes.

"There was not enough evidence to make any charges. Mind you, I did not *want* to charge him with plagiarism. I simply wanted to protect him from any possible trouble.

"But I was very alert after that. And I saw other passages that were familiar, but never enough for plagiarism to be a potential issue."

"And nothing was ever done about it?" Hayley asked.

"What could be done?" Max shrugged. "There are limits to what can be considered plagiarism, and Peter had, consciously or otherwise, stayed safely within the boundaries. But I admit I was quite disappointed after this."

"So, Peter actually did what he accused you of."

"Yes, it would seem so." Max frowned at Hayley. "And he suggested that I stole your book?"

"I can't remember if he actually said it or not," Hayley replied, "but comments were made, whether, as you said, 'consciously or otherwise,' that introduced the suspicion in my mind. I'm sorry, Max."

"There was another incident," Max said, shaking his head. "A few months ago, the history department held a fund-raiser, and I managed to arrange to have a few items from a local museum to be on display at various points around the auditorium. Peter helped me with the arrangements, and he strongly encouraged that I acquire a favorite piece of his from the museum, an exquisite dagger and sheath from about the eighth century AD.

"Unfortunately, our security measures were not as stringent as those of the museum itself. Somehow, that evening, that dagger and sheath disappeared. As that was the sole piece that was taken, Peter was very apologetic about pushing me to get it for the fund-raiser.

"Aside from the humiliation and the bad publicity, the university did not suffer for it. I fear I lost some credibility in my circle, but the insurance paid for the item. And again, the case was never solved.

"As for Peter, my suspicions were aroused once again, but I had no proof of any wrongdoing. I still do not, but I do not trust him, especially after these most recent accusations."

"No, of course not," Hayley replied, her eyebrows puckered together. Then, one of her previous suspicions resurfaced. "One thing I'm curious about. When I came here on Friday, I saw you sitting with a man, and you were showing him copies of pages from my book."

"Yes, as I told you, he was a professor here. In fact, he was *my* professor. I was consulting him on a couple of phrases, and how they should be translated."

Hayley sighed and nodded.

"I'm sorry I didn't trust you."

"No, please do not give it another thought. I would be very careful about Peter, though, if I were you."

"Well, it appears the damage is already done." Then, she cocked her head as she thought of something. "Hold on, though, I was with Peter when the book was stolen. He took me out to lunch today." Hayley saw that look cross Max's face, but now she understood why. "Don't worry, I accepted his invitation in order to break it off with him."

"Ah." Hayley couldn't tell if the look on his face now expressed satisfaction or relief. "Well, he was with me a good portion of the night during the fund-raiser. I think, if my suspicions are right, that he has a helper."

"Come to think of it, I did tell him last night on the phone that you had returned the book to me."

"So he arranged to get you away from home, and somebody else did the actual break-in."

"That bastard!" Hayley said under her breath.

Chapter 30

eynold Baron von Hoffmann was furious. This day was not going well at all. Having to pay all that money to that musician or magician, whatever he was, just so those vermin could get their children back. They weren't his responsibility. He shouldn't have to pay the bulk of that price, especially since his own son wasn't even taken.

But what really made him angry, even more than having to pay the money, was the way he was compelled to do it. The way old Mayor Hildebrandt spoke to him! He gave no regard whatsoever to Reynold's rank and standing in the community! Threatening to reveal his relationship with Katarina to the Duke. Reynold should have just drawn his sword and run him through right then!

And that piper! The way he just started playing his flute and unceremoniously sent him away along with all the townspeople! While he had to admit it was an intriguing ability, to just dismiss him like that was insulting.

The more he thought about it, the angrier he became. He had just been riding aimlessly since then, fuming over his appalling treatment. At first, he had been unable to resist the sudden desire to leave. He had simply wheeled his horse around and left. But once he got out of earshot of the melody, the urge had worn off, and he was just left with the anger.

The way he saw it, there were two people that needed attention, that rotund little toad Hildebrandt, and the piper. Hildebrandt would require a little finesse. Perhaps tonight, in private. But the piper, he could deal with him now and get back the money. And that flute could certainly be a useful item. And he would end up being seen as a hero, besides, ridding the town of a vile enemy!

Turning his horse around, he rode back toward the cave.

§

Cort and the piper were the only ones left back at the cave. Cort hoped to be able to free the children, and the piper's music had no effect on him, but still, every time he attempted to loosen

154

a stone, the piper was beside him, threatening him with a dagger. Cort saw him as an annoyance, like a persistent mosquito.

Cort remembered the pickaxe that Abelard had given him, and he turned and picked it up, catching a glimpse of Abelard's broken and contorted body on the rocks below. He sighed and turned toward the sealed entrance of the cave. The piper lunged toward him with his dagger, but Cort easily knocked it away with the head of the pickaxe.

Remembering the last battle he engaged in, he knew it would be such an easy matter to dispatch this poorly-armed musician. But Cort had turned his back on that life, and on violence in general. For the children, though, he thought, and for Abelard, he might make an exception.

But perhaps he wouldn't need to. He caught a glimpse of Bergh's father, Baron von Hoffmann, creeping up stealthily behind the piper, sword in hand.

Cort, of course, couldn't hear a thing. Everything was as silent as the tomb. But, apparently, von Hoffmann broke a twig or dislodged a pebble. The piper suddenly turned toward him, slipping his dagger back into its scabbard. He put the flute to his lips and began playing, and Cort immediately noticed a change in von Hoffmann.

The Baron turned his attention to Cort, his sword now pointed at Cort's chest. Cort held the pickaxe at the ready, his grip loose and easy. When von Hoffmann lunged at him, he easily knocked the sword away, careful to not injure Bergh's father. But von Hoffmann continued undeterred as the piper kept playing his tune.

After several unsuccessful attempts at Cort's life, with Cort almost effortlessly resisting them, he was becoming irritated at the delay. The children were trapped behind a wall of rocks, and he was wasting too much time.

§

Roland, Duke of Saxony, rode with a determined expression. Angry lines were set deeply in his face. Having finally completed his business, he had arrived back at his country home near

Hamelin, hoping to relax a bit. Katarina had seemed happy to see him.

He thought it was odd, though, when he found a pair of men's gloves in their bedroom, gloves that were not his. When questioned about it, Katarina denied any knowledge of them. Indeed, she suddenly seemed nervous, casting about for any reason why the gloves might be there.

Leaving her, he went downstairs and questioned the staff. Many of them seemed nervous and anxious, as well, though they didn't speak up. One young lady in the housekeeping staff, though, Greta, seemed eager to talk, so he had taken her into another room. Her face took on a solemn expression that seemed to belie her eagerness to talk.

"I'm afraid, Your Grace," she said, "there has been a man who has called fairly regularly on the Duchess in your absence." She leaned forward a little, as if taking him into her confidence. "It's my understanding that he has even spent the night on a few occasions." In her enthusiasm to reveal this information to him, she seemed oblivious to his growing anger and consternation.

"Who is this man?" the Duke asked.

"Baron von Hoffmann, Your Grace." The Duke sucked in a quick breath at the name.

"Reynold?" he replied incredulously. Reynold von Hoffman had sought his guidance on numerous business matters, and the Duke had taken him into his home as a friend. Such a betrayal came as a shock.

"Yes, Your Grace."

"Thank you, Greta," he said, dismissing her. She smiled absently and did a bit of a curtsy, then turned. "Oh, Greta," he said as an afterthought, having ascertained her love of gossip, "do you know anything of Baron von Hoffmann's schedule? You don't happen to know where he is now, do you?"

"Nothing for certain, Your Grace. But it's my understanding that nearly everyone with a child is at the cave by the river."

His expression told her that there was a lot of which he was unaware, so she related what had transpired over the last couple of days.

What a strange and ridiculous story that was. But he didn't spend much of his ride thinking about that. Reynold Baron von Hoffmann, his erstwhile friend, and Katarina occupied the forefront of his mind. Thinking of that man in his bed, with his wife, nearly drove him mad! He needed time to decide what to do about Katarina. He loved her, or at least, he had. He didn't know for certain what he felt for her anymore.

But he did know how he felt about von Hoffmann.

Chapter 31

Max typed out a brief message on his phone, "*Komm in mein Büro,*" and sent it to Peter.

"I suppose I may as well get back to cleaning while I wait," he said.

"Of course," Hayley said. "I'll help you."

When the door finally opened, Max was down on the floor gathering papers that had been strewn from his file cabinet, very near where he had been when Hayley arrived.

"*Scheiße, was ist das?*" Peter asked as he came in. Then, he saw Hayley working closer to the desk, and his face suddenly drooped. "What's going on?" he asked, switching to English to include Hayley.

"Have a seat, Peter," Max said quietly as he neatened the stack of random papers. He picked it up and placed it on a corner of his desk to sort later. Hayley picked up a stack of books and placed them on a shelf. She leaned against the cabinet that stood under the shelves as Max sat in the chair at his desk. Peter eased himself down into the chair, looking expectantly from one to the other.

As Max stared unblinking at Peter, Hayley almost expected him to say, "Ve haf vays uff making you talk." His cold stare was having an effect on Peter. Peter glanced nervously at Hayley who, despite her usual happy nature, also managed a pretty cold stare.

Finally, without a word being spoken, Peter nodded.

"Okay," he said quietly, "you know." He sighed and lowered his head. "God, I'm so sorry." Hayley almost believed him. Peter looked at her again and, as if he could see that bit of doubt on her face or read her thoughts, he said, "Really! I didn't want any of this."

"Any of what?" Hayley asked.

Peter glanced at Max again and, as if recognizing a more receptive audience, he addressed his story almost entirely to Hayley, though he still kept his head down.

"I come from something of a crime family," he sighed. "My father runs an import/export business in Philadelphia. He deals mainly in antiquities on the black market. I never wanted anything to do with it. And for most of my life, I managed to stay out of it."

"Really?" Hayley asked, her voice a bored monotone. "So you're Michael Corleone?"

"Basically, yes," Peter nodded. "And because of it, I've always been a major disappointment to my father. Do you know what it's like to not want any part of something your family spent years building?"

Hayley glanced at Max, remembering his background, having turned his back on being a lawyer like his father and brothers. His face, though, remained impassive as he listened to Peter's story.

"Anyway," Peter continued, "apparently there were rumors about a medieval-era book in Hannover."

"What rumors?" Max asked.

"I don't know," Peter insisted. "I've never been involved in the business. I don't know how it works. But I know my father has people all over the place, always looking for something that could turn a profit.

"So, as I understand it," he glanced nervously at Hayley before continuing, "they arranged a caretaker for the invalid who supposedly owned it."

"My father," Hayley said coldly. Peter nodded.

"This caretaker was actually one of my father's brothers, Roderick, and apparently he would spend their time together trying to get your father to talk about it, to reveal where it was. But he wouldn't say anything about it. I guess after a while, they decided they needed to come up with a different plan.

"My father was well aware of my love of German history. I was working on my doctorate at Penn State at the time. Somehow, he arranged for me to be able continue my studies at Stotzheim University. With their world-class history and antiquities department, he knew I'd jump at the chance to transfer here.

"In exchange, I was to keep my eyes and ears open. My father figured that, if anyone found a vintage German book they wanted appraised or translated, if it surfaced in town in any way," he glanced up again at Hayley, "Stotzheim is where they would come." He sighed again. "To my shame, I agreed. I couldn't resist.

"Well, several months passed and I never heard anything. I kind of forgot about the deal and just enjoyed my time here.

"Then," he glanced up at Hayley again, "you showed up last week with the book. That brought it all back and, as agreed, I reported it to my father." He kneaded his eyes anxiously. "I hated doing it. I hated even being involved in it, and I regretted ever making that deal with him." He held Hayley's eyes. "Especially as I started getting to know you."

"So, where's my book?" Hayley asked, apparently unmoved by his story.

"It's at my apartment," he replied quietly. "Josef, the man who acquired it for me met me just after lunch."

"Acquired it?" Hayley echoed, her eyebrow arched in a dangerous angle.

"Stole it," Peter corrected. He looked up at Max. "I'm so sorry about your office," he said in an imploring tone. Then, he looked up at Hayley. "And about—"

"About what?" Hayley asked when he didn't finish.

Peter looked back down as if he couldn't hold her gaze.

"I learned later that Roderick . . . when he couldn't coax any information from your father about the book," he paused, taking a long, deep breath, "shot him. Apparently,

160

the thinking was that they could coax the book out by an heir. But they hadn't counted on your father being completely estranged from his family.

"I guess your father struggled, but in his condition, he wasn't able to fight Roderick off completely. The shot didn't kill him, but it was pretty devastating. Still, it took your father a long time to finally go."

Hayley quickly wiped the tears forming in her eyes before Peter looked back up at her.

"Roderick probably would have finished him off, except that someone came into the house right then and he had to make a run for it."

"Elsbeth's friend," Hayley said.

"Hayley," Peter beseeched, "I really am so sorry. I didn't know anything about that until I had been here a while. I guess my father thought that might deepen my resolve, by making me an accessory."

"What about Henry," Max asked, "my previous assistant?"

Peter looked at Max and rubbed his eyes again, wiping the tears on his pants.

"I don't know," he shook his head. "It wouldn't surprise me if my father arranged it, but he never told me about that."

"My book is at your apartment?" Hayley asked, struggling to keep any emotion from her voice.

"Yes," Peter replied quietly. "I'll go get it."

"And give you an opportunity to have second thoughts and run off with her book?" Max asked. "I do not think so. I will come with you."

"It's my book," Hayley added. "I'm coming, too."

Chapter 32

Please," Cort shouted, "don't make him do this!"

But the piper kept playing his tune, and von Hoffmann kept advancing on Cort. As the piper's melody intensified, so did von Hoffmann's attacks. Jabbing and swinging his sword with increased fury, Cort was having a difficult time fending off the blows. The blade had already found him a couple of times, a glancing blow above his eye, and a cut on his shoulder. Neither wound was serious, but they were painful. And the cut on his forehead kept bleeding into his eye, increasing the difficulty of his defense.

If this had been a typical battle against a typical enemy, Cort could have dispatched him easily. But he was Bergh's father. In this precarious setting, Cort didn't want to risk injuring him, much less killing him.

He realized that his only hope was to make his way to the piper and get that flute away from him, one way or another. But between him and the piper was von Hoffmann, engaged in his tireless effort to kill him.

§

The Duke was met with a strange tableau when he arrived at the location that Greta had directed him to. Several of the townspeople were milling about looking up the hill. Following their gaze, he saw the celebrated former warrior, Cort Rottweill wielding a pickaxe, and doing battle with von Hoffmann. Several paces away was the person that Greta had described, playing his flute, almost as if he was directing the battle.

The Duke realized that Cort was not really trying to best von Hoffmann, and he began thinking that it was as if von Hoffmann was being saved for him. The longer he watched, the angrier he became, remembering the betrayal of his friend with his wife. His blood boiling, he reached for the crossbow slung from his saddle. He placed his foot in the stirrup and pulled the string back until it caught on the nut and locked in place. Slipping a bolt into the groove, he lifted the crossbow and sighted up the hill.

§

Cort had to time it just right. If he could knock von Hoffmann's sword away with the pickaxe, at just the right angle, he could move von Hoffmann out of the way and rush the piper. The terrain was dangerous, but he was pretty sure he could make it to him and slay the murderous fiend, silencing his flute before von Hoffmann could do any more damage.

During the last several minutes, he had watched von Hoffmann closely, recognizing from his stance whether he was going to thrust or swing, and which direction. Finally, he saw the move he was hoping for as von Hoffmann placed his left foot forward a bit. Gripping the pickaxe handle tightly, he angled it upward as von Hoffmann swung his sword to slice downward.

Before he could finish the arc, though, von Hoffmann's face contorted in surprise and pain, the sword poised at the top of his swing. Momentarily confused, Cort saw a crimson stain spreading downward on his shirt, from the point of a crossbow bolt protruding from von Hoffmann's chest.

As von Hoffmann fell, Cort looked around for his killer. He saw the Duke on his horse down below, the crossbow in his hand. The piper turned and looked around as well, alarmed that his instrument, von Hoffmann, had been killed. He noticed the Duke at the same time and began playing another tune.

While Cort couldn't hear the tune, he could see what was happening. Still sitting astride his horse, the Duke placed his foot in the stirrup of the crossbow, cocking it again. He placed another bolt in the groove and lifted the weapon.

Cort couldn't wait. He had to do it now, before the Duke's deadly accuracy found his new target. The piper was several meters away from him, over rough and uneven ground, on a slope strewn with loose dirt and rocks. Running toward him could be a dangerous endeavor. His decision was immediate.

The piper looked back and forth between the Duke and Cort, keeping watch over both of them. As he turned toward the Duke, Cort swung the pickaxe back and let it fly, hoping to, at the very least, knock the piper off balance and give Cort time to wrest the flute from him. He let go just as the Duke squeezed the trigger of his crossbow.

The pickaxe flew through the air, arcing gracefully end-over-end as the bolt flew toward Cort. Cort's last-minute forward momentum meant that the bolt only left a painful slice in his side on its way past.

The piper was not so fortunate. The point of the head of the pickaxe swung around and embedded itself in the piper's back. As he blew his last note, blood sprayed from his mouth and gurgled into the flute, muting the note and finally silencing the deadly instrument.

The piper fell face-down and slid a couple of meters down the hill on the loose gravel. Cort dropped to his knees gasping for breath, as the anxious townspeople rushed up the path.

Chapter 33

The apartment building was a large white-fronted block with fairly small, regularly-spaced windows, less than five minutes away from the university. It didn't look like much from the outside.

The three of them got out of Max's Audi, and Peter opened the front door. As they entered the building's foyer, the luxury became a little more apparent, the walls lined with oak wainscoting. A table stood near the front door holding a large flower arrangement.

"My apartment is just down here," Peter said.

He led them through the foyer and into a hallway. He fished his keys out of his pocket and unlocked a door, leading them inside. Despite the sun shining outside, it was dark in the apartment.

Max closed the door behind them, and he and Hayley followed Peter.

"I don't remember closing the drapes," Peter mumbled as he switched on a light. Hayley was shocked when the light illuminated the room. It was not lavish, but quite nice. Decorated with old German weaponry – swords, shields, pikes, poleaxes – it wasn't the décor that shocked her, but the man sitting in the chair waiting for them.

"Uncle Roderick," Peter exclaimed. "What are you doing here?"

The man's face was cold and hard, his icy blue eyes moving back and forth in his head as he took in everything. Looking at him, Hayley had a hard time picturing him as her father's caretaker.

She could easily see him as his killer, though.

"Josef reported that he got the book," Roderick replied in a soft voice that was pitched higher than Hayley would have expected. "I've come to get it from you."

"Oh, okay." Peter nervously glanced at Hayley and Max.

"Who are your friends?"

"This is one of my professors," Peter replied haltingly, and he locked eyes for a moment with Hayley, "and – his girlfriend."

"Hmm," Roderick said, narrowing his eyelids. "She looks a lot like Hayley Hoffmann." Peter's shoulders sagged. "You're not trying to pull anything, are you Peter?" He reached a hand inside his blazer and pulled out a handgun.

Hayley stiffened and sucked in a quick breath. Without a word, Max quietly stepped in front of her.

"No, Uncle Roderick," Peter said, sighing heavily. "What would I be trying to pull? We're family."

"So, what made you think it was a good idea to bring them here?"

"I didn't. They just figured out what happened, and they *made* me bring them here."

"They made you? Are they armed?"

"No, but they threatened to turn me over to the police if I didn't give them the book back."

"You son of a bitch," Hayley growled, frowning at Peter. He glanced at her, then turned back to Roderick.

"Well, that complicates things a little," Roderick said. "We'll have to get rid of them."

"Keep an eye on them," Peter said. "I'll go and get the book."

Peter rushed past Roderick down a short hallway into his bedroom, and Hayley could see him open the closet door and step into it. She looked back at Roderick who was watching her and Max, his expression relaxed into almost a smile. Still slumped in the chair, Hayley had a feeling he wasn't really as relaxed as he looked.

She looked around at all the ancient weapons, wondering how she could safely get to one of them. Then, she wondered, if she *could* get her hands on one, could she use it? She had never been violent, never raised her hand in anger at anyone. With her heart thrashing her ribs from the inside, she noticed that Max was still in his protective stance in front of her, and was probably trying to calculate similar action.

A movement in her peripheral vision caught her eye as Peter emerged from the closet holding a cloth-wrapped bundle. He hesitated, looking around. Then, he moved to a different part of the room, disappearing from her view.

A moment later, he reappeared in the doorway, but he stopped and closed his eyes, standing completely still, aside from the heavy breathing, which he struggled to steady. Then, he started through the hallway back towards the living room, holding the book in front of him. Hayley thought she saw the glint of metal under the book.

As he came back into the living room, Roderick stood up to face him. With Peter's back to her, Hayley couldn't see everything that transpired, but she got a pretty good idea when she saw his right hand move quickly forward. She saw a pained expression on Roderick's face as he fell down onto the floor.

Peter stood there looking down at his uncle for a moment, his shoulders rising and falling with each panicked breath. Finally, he heaved a heavy sigh and turned toward Hayley and Max. As he approached them, he placed the 1300-year-old German dagger on top of the cloth-wrapped book. He held it out toward Max, his face looking almost relieved that it was over.

Of course, it wasn't over. He had killed his uncle, and deprived his father of the multi-million-dollar book. He would still have to answer for that, whether to his father or the authorities, but he still seemed relieved as Max took the bundle from him.

His relief turned to shock in an explosive instant when a shot rang out behind him. He fell forward and Max tried to ease him down to the floor, and Hayley saw Roderick lying on the floor, the gun still in his hand. He struggled to aim again, his hand shaking, and the muzzle followed Max downward.

Hayley ran toward him, and as she did, Roderick tried to move the gun toward her, but she reached him first. She kicked his hand, sending the gun sliding across the floor.

She heard Max behind her, speaking to someone on his phone, apparently to Germany's equivalent to 911. She was frantic for Peter, but she kept her eyes on Roderick. The threat was fading, though, as Roderick lay his head down on his still outstretched arm. As Hayley watched, he exhaled, his body appearing to deflate and shrink a little as his body settled against the floor. Then, he was still.

She had never watched a person die before, and she shuddered a little. Now that he was dead, she turned and ran back toward Max who was still on the phone. She couldn't understand what he was saying, but he appeared to be examining Peter and relating his findings to the person on the phone.

Peter was breathing, his head turned a little so he could see Hayley, but his eyes seemed to have trouble focusing. Hayley found that to be the case with hers, too, as they filled with tears.

She knelt down beside Peter, taking his hand, and she could barely feel the pressure as he tried to squeeze.

"I'm sorry about . . . so many things," he whispered, straining to get it out. "I'm not sorry . . . about the time I spent . . . with you."

He looked as if he had a brief moment of clarity as his eyes focused on Hayley, and he smiled. Then, he was still.

Feeling his hand go slack in her hand, Hayley let out a wail that caused Max to pause in speaking to the person on the phone. He leaned forward and looked at Peter. Seeing his stillness and his distant stare, he sighed and spoke quietly into the phone.

"*Er ist tot.*"

Still holding Peter's hand, Hayley didn't hear the two-tone siren approaching. She barely noticed Max kneeling beside her and holding her tightly against his chest, rocking her in his arms. It was only when the emergency responders entered the apartment and Max pulled her away from Peter to give the EMTs room that she became aware again of her surroundings.

Then, she buried her face in Max's chest and cried.

Chapter 34

he Duke pushed his way up the hill and jostled through the people. When the townspeople saw who it was, they parted, their heads bowed, to allow him to pass. He came to a stop beside Cort.

"Young man," he said, "I am so sorry!" There was no response, and the Duke knelt beside Cort, touching his shoulder. Cort turned and recognized him. "I'm sorry," the Duke said, "I forgot you were deaf." He noticed the blood soaking Cort's tunic from the wound. "I apologize for that," he said. "I had no control over what I was doing."

"I know, Your Grace," Cort replied graciously. "It's alright. I'm fine."

It was only then that Cort noticed the people crowding around him. Then, he remembered the children.

"Excuse me, Your Grace," he said as he stood up and stepped carefully toward the piper's body, slipping a little with each step. He gripped the end of the pickaxe handle, and he kicked it near the head, dislodging the point from the corpse. He saw a bag on the ground attached by a drawstring to the piper's belt, and he yanked it free.

He made his way back up toward the cave, and he saw Mayor Hildebrandt at the front of the crowd. Cort handed the money bag to him.

"This can be given back to the people," he said, and the Mayor smiled and nodded.

It took an hour or so of prying and chipping away at the rocks, but by midafternoon, Cort managed to open a hole through the rocks into the darkness of the cave. When they saw it, several of the townspeople rushed forward to relieve him and began pulling at the stones, widening the opening.

Cort sat down against the trunk of a tree, catching his breath, as he saw the first of the children scramble through the opening. He smiled at the cheerful reunions, and sighed at a couple of bittersweet ones, as he saw Abelard's daughter emerge to find only her tearful mother waiting for her.

Somebody had moved von Hoffmann's body off the path, and Cort saw Bergh leaning on his crutches looking down at him. There were tears in his eyes, but aside from that, his face was indecipherable.

After a few minutes, Cort pushed himself up and went to the boy, kneeling beside him. Bergh looked up at him, and the tears finally found enough weight to roll down his cheeks. He let go of his crutches and threw his arms around Cort's neck.

The warrior held him, letting him cry as long as he needed to. After a few minutes, Cort gathered up Bergh's crutches in one hand and picked up the boy in his other, starting down the path toward home.

§

Cort saw his neighbor waving to him as he and Bergh neared his cottage. Bergh was on his feet now, swinging along on his crutches.

"Christoph," Cort greeted him, "are you well?"

"I am," Christoph replied, "and so is Brenner. Thanks to you, we have our son back!" Cort smiled. "And thanks to your friend, we have our daughter." Cort's smile turned to confusion.

"I don't understand. Is Emelyne alright?"

"Yes, she is. Thanks to Elysande." He motioned for Cort to come inside.

Cort looked down at Bergh, and they turned to go into the cottage. As his eyes gradually adjusted to the relative darkness, Cort saw Ely sitting in a chair, leaning against the table, as she was being attended to by Emelyne and Frieda, Christoph's wife. Their son, Brenner, was there too, but didn't seem to know what to do. Seeing someone closer to his age, he went to Bergh and began talking with him, as Ely looked up.

"Cort," she said, looking alarmed at the blood on his head and his tunic. She pushed herself up from the table, and she swayed a little unsteadily. Cort rushed to her, taking her in his arms. He held her for a moment, feeling a shiver despite her warmth, then he helped her back down into the chair. They didn't see the furtive smile that Christoph and Frieda exchanged. "I'm fine," Ely said. "Just a little overwhelmed."

"Yes," Christoph confirmed, "she had quite an adventure of her own."

With a glance at Emelyne, he related, without too much detail, what had transpired during Cort's absence.

"They were the same men who—" she glanced at the boys who were involved in a conversation of their own, exchanging their experience that morning with the piper. Ely lowered her voice a little. "They were the men who raped and beat me."

"I suppose I would be overwhelmed myself," Frieda said shakily. Christoph raised his eyebrows and nodded.

"She's a good one," he said quietly, leaning closer to Cort. "You had better hold on to her."

Cort looked up with surprise as Christoph gave a knowing wink.

Chapter 35

"That is the last one," Max said as he straightened up and stretched his back. Hayley looked at all the boxes he had carried out for her, lined up in front of her garage.

"Thank you so much, Max," Hayley said.

"It is my pleasure," he said in his typical soft voice, and bowing his head toward her a bit in a gesture so formal that Hayley couldn't help but laugh. She went to him and put her arms around him, kissing him. Max seemed confused at her laughter, but he smiled and returned the kiss.

The boxes of trash had already been hauled away. As for the items that were suitable for charitable donation, Hayley had found a service that would pick up the boxes, and they were coming in the morning. Max had offered to carry them out from the basement and the attic for her.

In the last few weeks, they had spoken occasionally about Peter, but mostly, their thoughts were to themselves. Their thoughts of him were often a confusing mix of criminal, unethical, personable and, in Hayley's case, romantic, and it was just easier to keep them inside.

They had spoken of him frequently, of course, when the police investigation was going on. But the clues were abundant and the case was wrapped up fairly quickly.

Peter had been well-liked in the university, and his violent death came as a shock to many. Max decided to take some time off, not only for himself, but to be with Hayley and help her through the difficult time. She was grateful and seemed to respond well to him being close.

"Why don't you sit down and rest?" Hayley suggested. She had set up a couple of lawn chairs in the shade of the trees in front of the house, and she had just brought out a couple of bottles of *Franziskaner Weissbier*, placing them in the holders in the armrests of the chairs.

"Oh, my dear," he said as he settled into one of the chairs, "you are too good to me."

"I'm too good to you?" Hayley echoed in a disbelieving tone. "I just made you move tons of stuff out of my house."

"No," Max said, vigorously shaking his head, "I volunteered to do that, just because it was you. This is a bonus," and he took the bottle out of the holder and drained half of it, sighing heavily as he swallowed. Hayley smiled as she watched him, and she took a discreet swallow of her own beer.

"You really do have a lovely place here," Max said, looking around again at the house and the grounds.

"Thank you," Hayley said. "Apparently, my father had good taste in women and real estate. Max smiled and looked at Hayley.

"Has your mother come to terms, yet, with your decision to stay here?"

"Not yet," Hayley replied, letting her head fall back as a cool breeze blew across them. "I think it helps that I'll be going back there for some of my things, and to get my house in order. So it's not like she'll never see me again."

"Are you certain it is what you want?" Max asked.

"I am," she smiled. "For now, at least. My mother is in Denver," she made a gesture with both hands as if she were weighing two items, "and my father and my heritage are here. As you know, I never really knew my father, so I have a lot to learn. My fancy-schmancy car is here, Elsbeth is here, this beautiful house is here."

Max turned and looked at her, raising an eyebrow.

"And, of course, you're here," Hayley laughed. She reached over and placed her hand on the side of his face, and he leaned his head against it. He really was a dear and thoughtful man, and Hayley held his gaze for a few moments.

As sometimes happened, Peter's face appeared, as if superimposed over Max's, but Hayley was becoming more adept at pushing it away. Her brief time with Peter had been romantic and turbulent, and in the end, dangerous. She knew she had made the wise decision where Peter and Max were concerned, but Peter was still there at times. The choice he had made at the end made her memory of him more confusing and poignant. Still, from a cold and analytical standpoint, as well as a heartfelt one, she was happy with her choice.

Max was proving to be a stable and calming influence in her sometimes unsettled and blustery life.

"Have you decided what you want to do with the book?" Max asked. Hayley sighed and put her head back again.

"No," she groaned. "Thanks to that appraisal you had done, I know it's worth ten and a half million euros, but I don't need that kind of money. I'll have rent coming in from my house back in Denver. And thanks to that trust that you were clever enough to find, I have more than enough to live very comfortably on."

A cursory look at the other two books in Hayley's wine cellar had revealed that Baldric Hoffmann had indeed given thought to Hayley in his later years. One of the books was an old financial guide, and despite the dry and stodgy nature of the text, Max had, after consultations with a financial expert, discovered that the sheet of paper slipped into its pages was based on a law that had not changed in hundreds of years.

Hayley's father had created a trust fund for Hayley to be made available on her thirtieth birthday. After consulting with the lawyers and bankers named in the document, Max found that there was enough to support Hayley comfortably for the rest of her life.

"I was wondering how I was going to pay the property taxes on this place," she had said when he told her about it. Then, unable to contain her true excitement, she jumped up and down, laughing, and fell into Max's arms, just where he wanted her.

"I suppose donating the book to a museum, especially in Hamelin would be the most altruistic thing to do." She sighed again. "But it belonged to my father. I don't know, yet, why it was so important to him. Was there really a Baron von Hoffmann? Are we descended from him? Or is there some other, more virtuous connection to it? Or is there any connection at all?"

She turned to Max.

"Max, what should I do?"

He smiled at her and shook his head. He didn't know what would be the best thing for her to do. At this point, he didn't care anything about the book. He was just glad to be here, a part of her life.

Chapter 36

To Cort's surprise, he asked Ely that evening if she would marry him. To her surprise, Ely said yes. They were married in a simple ceremony a couple of days later.

Ely wore one of the dresses that Bergh had acquired for her from his mother. Due to her past, she felt unworthy of a religious ceremony, but Mayor Hildebrandt was happy to officiate.

Ely was not immediately accepted by the people of Hamelin. Many knew of her past, but they also knew of her attempt to put it behind her. A few of the nuns spoke up in her behalf. And when the townspeople heard the tale of how Ely saved Emelyne and killed her attacker, she gained the respect of many.

Hans' accomplices were not seen again.

Being now without a father or other relatives, Bergh was immediately taken in by Cort and Ely to be raised as if he was their own son. With the death of Reynold Baron von Hoffmann, his estate was passed on to Bergh. As Bergh was only twelve years old, though, Cort, as his legal guardian, took over the duties until whatever time Bergh had the ability or desire to carry them out.

The staff of the von Hoffmann home had their doubts about Cort as their new employer, and about Ely as the mistress of the house. In a short time, though, they won them over, gaining their loyalty and esteem. As a well-liked and respected citizen, Cort was likewise a fair and respected landlord.

Mayor Hildebrandt, as Cort had requested, distributed the money in the piper's money bag back to the people who paid it. He also took charge of disposing of the piper's body. He thought about just pitching him into the river, to eventually end up with the other rats. In the end, the Mayor had the body quietly buried in an unmarked location.

The piper's flute was never found.

www.ingramcontent.com/pod-product-compliance
Lightning Source LLC
Chambersburg PA
CBHW051821170626
46807CB00003B/971